Cover Copy

Traveling through time…for a Highlander.

With her dying breath, Katherine MacLean makes a wish inside a faerie circle, a wish that sends her traveling through time and into the arms of the warrior the fae have bound her soul to. She is the progeny of two great clans, MacLean and MacDonald, but with a vicious feud raging between them, she's called by the fae to unite and bring about some peace.

Highland warrior John MacDonald holds a piece of Katherine's soul and only through him can she survive. When Katherine escapes him to the enemy's land to see to the fae's mission, everything within him demands he make chase and protect her.

Once Katherine joins her MacLean kin, she discovers her mission is not quite as it seems. Can she find a way to claim the warrior her soul hungers for…without becoming the one who ignites the feud?

Books by Joanne Wadsworth

The Matheson Brothers Series
Highlander's Desire, Book One
Highlander's Passion, Book Two
Highlander's Seduction, Book Three
Highlander's Kiss, Book Four
Highlander's Heart, Book Five
Highlander's Sword, Book Six
Highlander's Bride, Book Seven
Highlander's Caress, Book Eight
Highlander's Touch, Book Nine
Highlander's Shifter, Book Ten
Highlander's Claim, Book Eleven
Highlander's Courage, Book Twelve
Highlander's Mermaid, Book Thirteen

Highlander Heat Series
Highlander's Castle, Book One
Highlander's Magic, Book Two
Highlander's Charm, Book Three
Highlander's Guardian, Book Four
Highlander's Faerie, Book Five
Highlander's Champion, Book Six
Highlander's Captive (Short Story)

Billionaire Bodyguards Series
Billionaire Bodyguard Attraction, Book One
Billionaire Bodyguard Boss, Book Two
Billionaire Bodyguard Fling, Book Three

Books by Joanne Wadsworth

Regency Brides Series
The Duke's Bride, Book One
The Earl's Bride, Book Two
The Wartime Bride, Book Three
The Earl's Secret Bride, Book Four
The Prince's Bride, Book Five
Her Pirate Prince, Book Six

Princesses of Myth Series
Protector, Book One
Warrior, Book Two
Hunter (Short Story - Included in Warrior, Book Two)
Enchanter, Book Three
Healer, Book Four
Chaser, Book Five

Highlander's Faerie

Highlander Heat, Book Five

Joanne Wadsworth

Highlander's Faerie
ISBN-13: 978-1-99-003426-8
Copyright © 2014, Joanne Wadsworth
Cover Art by Joanne Wadsworth
First electronic publication: December 2014

Joanne Wadsworth
http://www.joannewadsworth.com

AUTHOR'S NOTE:
This book is a work of fiction. The names, characters, places, and incidents are products of the writer's imagination or have been used fictitiously and are not to be construed as real. Any resemblance to persons, living or dead, actual events, locale or organizations is entirely coincidental. The author does not have any control over and does not assume any responsibility for third-party websites or their content.

Published in the United States of America

First digital publication: December 2014
First print publication: February 2015

Dedication

As a child I loved making wishes on the first star I saw at night, and to this day I still do. This one is for everyone who loves wishing too.

Acknowledgements

I have an incredibly supportive family who allow me so much time to write. Huge thanks go to my hubby, Jason, and kiddies, Marisa, Caleb, Cruise and Rocco. Hugs.

For my readers, I can't thank you enough for joining me, and taking this journey to where imagination and magic soar.

A Word From The Author

Each book within this *Highlander Heat* series is stand-alone, although for your reading pleasure you may wish to read Highlander's Magic book two, before this one as the two stories involve twin sisters traveling through time. Marie's story comes first in Magic, and now this one is Katherine's.

The Faerie Circle

The ruins of Dunyvaig Castle, on the Isle of Islay, Scotland, current day.

The full moon, a bright ball of eerie orange, hung low along the ocean's horizon and cast its glow over ghostly wisps of cloud floating across it. The wind rose, and inside Dunyvaig's faerie circle, Katherine MacLean huddled on the cold, damp grass, her knees drawn tight to her chest. Nine white stones standing six feet high and six feet apart surrounded her, while a tenth center stone, short enough to sit on but just as wide, shone marble smooth with her ancestor's silver amulet draped upon it. Mary MacLean's talisman had been engraved on one side with the MacLean clan crest, and on the reverse, the MacDonald crest. The piece had been gifted to Mary on the day she'd wed the MacDonald chief, and should have represented the time when the two great clans had finally come together in harmony. Instead the feud had become bitterer and raged across the Western Isles.

Even as Mary's kin had battled, she'd continued to wear the amulet as a firm reminder she belonged to both clans, until the day had come when Mary had decided nothing more could be done except to ask the faerie folk for aid. She'd stood in this circle and made a wish, asking the Guardians of Dunyvaig to aid her in bringing peace between her clans. They'd instructed her to bequeath her amulet to her eldest daughter, requesting it be passed down through the generations until it once again came into the possession of the eldest daughter born to a MacLean. That had taken over four-hundred years, but it was a gift Katherine's older twin sister, Marie, had held dear to her heart.

Marie had received the bestowment on her twenty-first birthday, and following it, Katherine and Marie had traveled halfway around the world, from Australia's Gold Coast to Scotland's mainland then by ferry to this beautiful isle. As the progeny of two bickering clans, they'd brought Mary's amulet home as she'd requested.

Then a mere week ago, Katherine had stood in this faerie circle with her sister and made a wish that had gone awry. That wish had lowered the veil and taken Marie away from her and far into the past.

Behind Katherine, high on the craggy hill, Dunyvaig's ruins tormented her. Those blocks of jagged stone lay so heartbreakingly cold and alone, as she'd been this past week without her sister. Rocking, she allowed her tears to trickle free. "Please," she cried out to the little folk, "I'll do whatever you ask of me. Grant me one more wish. Allow me to join my sister. She's all I have left in this world."

Pain speared through her and she slumped onto her side. Blood flowed down her neck from an open wound that had come out of nowhere. She grasped the edges, but her lifeblood poured through her fingers and soaked her red and blue tartan coat.

Vision blurring, she scrambled to the edge of the circle and hit a hazy barrier. Beyond the fog, the darkened waves of Lagavulin Bay rolled in with a pounding crash, and high on the hill, Dunyvaig Castle rose strong. Three stories high, its battlements topped fortified walls and candles glowed from the tower windows.

"Mary, you're no' to wander beyond the gates," a guardsman bellowed as he rushed across the top of the barbican.

A woman with a riot of red-gold curls swaying around her belly swollen with child hurried toward the circle and patted the sides. "The veil has risen," Mary called to the guard. Kneeling in her white gown, she peered within, right at Katherine. Softly, she murmured, "Please, whose presence do I feel? That of the fae?"

"I need your aid." Katherine fought to get to her knees and hammered the veil with what strength she had.

"I hear whispers from within." Mary searched the circle. "Guardians of Dunyvaig, I implore you. Marie has gone to battle for the Rhinns and I fear for her safety. She will perish if my brother's life is taken. Lachlan MacLean has yet to father her paternal line. If he dies, she dies."

"Mary, you have to send someone to Marie." She clutched her wounded neck.

"Aye, if that is what the fae ask of me, then that is what I shall do."

"I'm not one of the—"

"Ye must come inside, Mary." The guard strode out in a thick fur vest and breeches, his sword at his side. "'Tis late and the weather turns."

"Nay, I need a moment. I can sense the fae's presence." Mary bowed her head against the veil. "Please, show yourself to me."

"There is none there. Now come." The warrior helped Mary to her feet and gently led her back through the gates.

"Mary, stay. I—I—" Black spots danced before her eyes. No. She had to hold on.

"Katherine." A voice floated all around and a light shimmered. "I am one of the fae and have heard your wish. If your desire is to join your sister then you must survive. Your paternal ancestor is wounded, just as you are. Hold strong."

"I need Marie." She fought the descending fog.

"I know. You've always needed each other." Another voice, and not one she'd ever forget, not when it belonged to her late mother. She blinked and forced her vision to clear. A glowing form made of mist and moonlight materialized and took the shape of the woman who'd given birth to her, the woman she'd mourned since her death only a few months past.

"Mum? Am I dead?"

"No, but I'm here. Your father and I never wished to leave you and I've always been close, as is he."

Another form shimmered to radiant life next to her mother.

"Dad?" On her knees, she tried to grab them but met nothing but air.

Thunder rumbled all around and lightning hit the rippling waves of the bay with a sizzling crackle. The veil thinned and her parents and the faerie fluttered away.

The dark consumed her.

Katherine and Marie's Parents

Inside the faerie circle, a day later.

"We need to do something." Marianne MacDonald lowered to her knees in the faerie circle next to her husband. Her daughter was so close yet still beyond her touch, right where she'd fallen the day before. She called to the fae, "Marigold, please, we need you."

"I'm here." She shimmered into sight and kneeling, pressed her palm against Katherine's chest. "Wake, my child. 'Tis I, one of the fae."

Katherine stirred and coughed. Slowly, she opened her eyes then fumbled for the fae's hand. "Help me," she croaked.

"I have already promised to give you aid, although to survive your soul will need to be bound to another who already walks this Earth."

"Do something. Anything." Blood dribbled from Katherine's mouth.

"You will need to join your sister in the past. That is now your place. Look. She comes."

Marie snuck across the stony courtyard and passed under the arched entrance.

Marianne soaked in the sight of her firstborn child, as did her husband who gripped her hand.

"I'm here, Katherine." Marie slipped between two of the perimeter stones, knelt before the center stone and eyed Mary's amulet sitting upon it. "Where are you, sis?"

Katherine gurgled on blood and her eyes fluttered shut as she breathed her last.

"They can't see each other. Quickly, do something," Marianne urged the fae. "Katherine can't die."

Marigold closed her eyes and murmured, "I hereby bind Katherine MacLean's soul to the one man who should have always been hers. He lives in this time, her warrior protector. Send a piece of her inner light to him, so that he might guide and watch over her, throughout all time."

A bright light shimmered around Katherine's prone form and tendrils separated from her body and floated beyond the circle. As the fae swept her hands over Katherine, the wound on her neck closed and the blood drew away until not a drop remained. Marigold breathed into Katherine's mouth then stroked her cheek. "Wake, my child, but without fear. You shall no' remember what has happened here until you're ready."

Marianne held her breath.

Katherine gasped and dragged in precious air.

"'Tis done." Marigold nodded at Marianne. "In healing your daughter, her memories of the past day in this circle will be gone, but she will recall what is needed in time. 'Tis best that way."

Tears trickled down Marianne's cheeks. "Thank you."

"Come." Marigold drew her and Locky away. "We can no longer intervene or be seen."

"She needs to know we're here."

"Nay. For now, 'twill be too much for her to bear."

"Please, let Katherine come," Marie cried out to the fae as she thumped the short center stone. "I need her."

"I'm here." Katherine shook her groggy head and crawled closer to her sister. She swished her hand through Marie's form. "No. I can see you, but not touch you."

Marianne grasped her husband's hand. "They have to find each other, Locky."

"They will. Trust in the fae." He squeezed her hand in return.

"I can hear you, sis." Marie sagged forward. "I saw to Archie's wish. Lachlan MacLean lives and he's been taken by the king's men to Edinburgh as history has foretold. Our paternal line continues on. You and I will survive."

"Then come home to me. I'm between times."

"Marie!" Archie shouted her name as he raced down the trail, his white shirttails flying free behind him. The MacDonald warrior hit the edge of the circle, bounced off and slammed onto the ground. Stunned, he shook his head then staggered to his feet. "Hell, the veil's up."

"Take the amulet, sis." Katherine pleaded.

"Marie, is Katherine in there with you?" Archie shoved against the veil. "Dinnae go to her, no' yet. I need to hold you, one last time."

"Marie." Katherine clambered to her feet, her long blond hair whipping about her in the swirling breeze. "Every day since you disappeared into the past, I've returned and waited for you. I'm right here, and I've watched those ruins and wished for the castle to reappear. Pick up the amulet. It must be the only way you can get back to me."

"I don't want to leave him, but I'll never leave you." Marie wrapped shaky fingers around the amulet and slipped it over her head.

Katherine gasped and grabbed her sister as she appeared in full form before her. "Oh my goodness, you're back. I can finally touch you. You're real."

"We're together again." Marie mashed their wet cheeks

together.

"Archie!" Archie's brother raced down the trail, his warrior's sword at his side. "What's happened?"

"Marie's gone, John." Archie clutched the grass and ripped handfuls free. "She's gone."

"Then wish for Marie back, as you wished for her in the very beginning." John crouched beside Archie.

"This is what Marie wanted, to return to her sister. I willnae make her choose between her own kin and me." Archie seized his brother's arm. "I must give her up."

Katherine hugged Marie tight then looked into her eyes. "I can see Archie loves you."

"He has my heart." Marie peered at Archie, her gaze filled with such longing.

Katherine glanced between the warrior and her sister. "We should join them, Marie. There is nothing left for us in the future. Mum and Dad are gone. We have no other family." She swiped the talisman from around Marie's neck, clasped hands with her and wound the amulet around both their wrists. "Let's do this, but this time, we go together. You're not leaving me again."

"Are you sure?"

Marianne wrung her hands together. "Yes," she whispered to her daughters as she pressed them, "you must go together."

"It's been hard to live without our parents, so yes, I'm sure. Surely you don't want to lose another person you love too?" Katherine strode toward John and pressed her hand against the veil in front of him. "John, it's Katherine, Marie's sister. Tell Archie to make a wish, for both my sister and me."

"I hear you." The warrior rose and rested his hand over Katherine's. "Make a wish, Archie, for both of them. Katherine asks it of you."

"I'll try." Archie squeezed his eyes shut. "Guardians of Dunyvaig, I ask for a wish. For you to send me the woman who has stolen my heart and the one she holds closest to her. Bring them here, so we need never live apart again." He swept his hand through the air and Marie's amulet rose, breached the barrier and spun into his palm.

A wind rose and tunneled around Katherine and Marie, whipping their hair across their faces. Marie clutched hold of Katherine. "Don't let go of me, sis. If you do, you'll be in more trouble than it's worth."

"I'm holding on. Sisters, forever." Katherine peered back toward Marianne and Locky and smiled.

"Can she see us, Marigold?" Marianne touched her heart.

"Nay, and so too her memories of this past day in the circle are gone, but as kin, she senses your presence all the same. Look." The fae motioned toward the streaming tendrils of Katherine's essence which still swirled beyond the veil. They wisped around John and then absorbed into his body. "He is her warrior protector, the one always meant for her. He now holds a piece of her soul. The two are deeply bound."

The veil thinned and Katherine fell through the barrier and into John's arms.

"Katherine has made the right choice and lives." The fae smiled. "Now she must accept her fate and her new bond with her warrior. She cannae survive without him. To do so, will mean her ultimate death."

"Then that's a death I'll never allow." Marianne held firm to her words. She'd do whatever it took to ensure both her daughters' survival and that Katherine remembered all that had gone on within this circle. She couldn't be with them in life, but she would still safeguard their future happiness.

She'd watch over them as she always had.

Chapter 1

Dunyvaig Castle, MacDonald stronghold, 1590, two weeks following Katherine's arrival.

Katherine stood at her chamber window. Beyond the gates, the faerie circle remained quiet, bare of any breeze, and the amulet glinting in the moonlight upon the center stone where her sister had tossed it following their arrival into the past. Something within the circle called to her, demanding her return, just as her nightly dreams urged her to do the same.

She needed answers, and it was time. She grasped her burgundy skirts, strode out of her room and down the winding stairs. Hurrying, she bypassed the great hall, walked across the stony inner courtyard and under the arched entrance.

After taking a deep, fortifying breath, she stepped into the circle and stopped before the center stone. Slowly, reverently, she picked up the amulet wads whispered, "Guardians of Dunyvaig, why have you brought me here?"

A breeze lifted her hair and made it tickle her face.

"My child," a voice breathed. "I've been waiting for you, to give you the guidance you seek."

"Am I real? Nightmares assail me and I see my death here

in this circle, a death I don't remember."

"Katherine, you no longer belong to the future, but here in the past. Wear the amulet. 'Tis yours to hold and will provide safe passage as you return to your MacLean kin."

"I'm to travel to the Isle of Mull?" Her sister was here and now wed to a MacDonald, her MacLean clan's greatest enemy. "Marie is away on her honeymoon. I can't leave her."

"You and your twin are two halves of one whole, the beginning and the end. You must complete what your sister has set in motion. Keep your warrior protector close. To bring peace, you must unite."

"My warrior protector?"

"Aye, the man who is ever watchful, the one who caught you as you fell into this time."

She slowly turned. High on the castle's battlements, John MacDonald stood with one hand resting on his sword hilt and the sea breeze plastering his blue tunic to his broad chest. "He's one of Angus MacDonald's captains. He can't travel with me to Mull and enter the enemy's territory."

"Aye, he can, if he does so for you. If that is what it will take for you to see the truth, then that is what must be." The fae's voice drifted on the wind, moving farther away. "You, my child, are of both clans, but there is more you arena aware of. There is magic all around you. Simply open your eyes if you wish to see it, then draw on the touch of fae blood you hold deep within you. You must accept your place in this time if you wish to survive."

"Hold on. I have fae blood?"

All was eerily still and no answer came. The fae had gone, and just as quickly as she'd come. And drat it. She was still without answers. Were her nightmares real?

Hands shaking, she lifted the talisman's silver chain over her head and pressed the amulet against her heart. She had a mission, and the fae's words reverberated through her mind. *Keep your warrior protector close. To bring peace, you must unite.* Bringing some peace between the clans was what she longed for. A strange sense of rightness stole over her. As Marie had completed her mission and saved their paternal ancestor, so too, she'd complete hers. She wouldn't let the fae down.

She trod out of the circle and climbed the stairs to the battlements, toward the one man who never veered far from her side.

Ahead, John pushed away from the thick stone crenellation and arms crossed, observed her. "What were you doing in the circle?"

"Seeking advice." Only John, Archie and Mary knew the truth of how she and Marie had come to travel from the future here to the past. "I spoke to one of the fae."

"You must take care. Even as the little folk guard Dunyvaig, they also tinker and play."

She palmed the amulet at her neck. It's silver surface glimmered in the moonlight.

"Tell me why you hold Mary's talisman. 'Twas left in the circle for a reason." With one finger under her chin, John lifted her gaze to his. "You can always speak to me."

"I know." Warmth from his gentle touch rolled through her. "The fae told me this amulet is now mine to hold and will provide safe passage as I return to my MacLean kin."

"You were asked to travel to Duart Castle on the Isle of Mull?"

"Yes. I've been given a mission."

"Nay, I'll never allow you to step one foot on MacLean territory, mission or no'." He pressed her against the stone wall at her back, enclosing her fully in his heat. "The danger is too great. Tell me exactly what the fae said."

"That Marie and I are two halves of one whole, the beginning and the end. I'm to complete what my sister has set in motion. She also said to keep my warrior protector close. To bring peace, we must unite." She pushed against him but he budged not an inch. "John, don't go getting all muscly-man on me."

"Shh, take care with your strange words. Voices can travel along the battlements and the other guards are close." He eased one hand under her shoulders and the other behind her head, protecting her from the rough stone. "While Archie is away, you're my responsibility. Traveling to Mull willnae happen on my watch. They're the enemy."

"Your enemy, not mine. I'm a MacLean, in case you forgot." She wriggled her trapped hands free from between them and sighed. "The Chief of MacLean will father my paternal line, just as Mary MacDonald will give birth to my maternal one. I may be living in the past, but in truth, I've yet to be born. Even Mary wishes for peace between the clans."

"Of which you've assured me does no' happen for many years. If you attempt to bring about peace, then you'd be changing the future, something you and Marie are adamant against doing. Now enough of this talk of traveling to Mull. 'Tis late and you need your rest." He tucked her under his shoulder and led her toward the stairs.

"The fae wouldn't have asked me to travel to Duart Castle if I wasn't supposed to."

"Mayhap what the fae said is no' all you believe. Consider their words well." He called out to the guardsman in the gatehouse, "Lower the portcullis. Secure the keep for the night."

The portcullis within the stone-arched entrance lowered, its clunky chains reverberating throughout the keep.

"I'm twenty-one, John. You can't demand I go to bed just because that suits you."

"I can and I did."

He was so frustrating.

"You also don't need to watch over me as intensely as you do." In the past fortnight, she'd barely slept, her dreams always swirling with darkness and death. Her cries had woken John that first night and ever since, he'd slept in her room, watching over her. "I'm not a child."

"I'm well aware." He opened the door and motioned her into the great hall.

"I spoke to the fae about my nightmares."

"You did?" He lifted one eyebrow. "And…"

"She said I no longer belonged to the future, but here in the past. Not much of an answer."

"Well, I agree you belong here, although I wish you'd speak to me of what awakens you at night."

"I'm sorry." She shook her head. "Perhaps it's my grief manifesting. I'm not sure. All I know is I miss them."

"Your parents?"

"Yes." Losing her mother to cancer a few short months ago had near broken her heart, as it had her sister's, particularly when it had come so close on the heels of their father's passing the year before. "Don't you miss your parents?"

His father had died on the battlefield the year he'd turned eighteen, and his mother on the day she'd given birth to him and Archie. How awful. He'd never even gotten to know his own mother.

"I think of them constantly. 'Tis best to allow only the good memories to surface." He guided her upstairs to the third floor, ushered her into her chamber and shut the door. Crouched before the hearth, he tore strips of bark from a log and brought a flame to life striking flint with his dagger. A fire soon blazed and spread its heat through the room. Hands dusted, he rose and crossed to the navy corner padded chair he'd slept in these past two weeks and plumped the pillow. With a deep sigh, he removed his sword belt, set it against the side of the chair then tucked a loose blue shirttail back into his black leather pants.

"I wish the nightmares would stop. I hate that I'm keeping you from your bed."

"Until they cease, I'll remain at your side. Do you need me

to unlace your gown?"

"Yes, please." She turned her back and he stepped in behind her. Holding the burgundy velvet bodice to her chest, she smiled over her shoulder at him. "In the future, one doesn't need this kind of help when undressing."

"Do you miss your men's trews?" A teasing glint lit his eyes as he scooped her hair and slid it to one side.

"They're called jeans, and in the twenty-first century, men and women both wear them, and yes, I do miss them." She'd fallen through the veil in her favorite skinny jeans and quite shocked John when she'd removed her tartan red and blue woolen coat to uncover them. "It's amazing to see how proficient you're getting at this task, although sleeping in my chamber must be giving your single status a knock."

"Single status? Another interesting term of yours." Chuckling, his breath puffed warmly against her back as he exposed her skin. "All here are aware of your nightmares and that I must maintain a vigil at your bedside. Your good name remains intact."

"My good name doesn't worry me."

"It should." A frown furrowed his brow.

"Well, I didn't mean it quite like that. It's just I'm here in the past and I have to be so careful. I can't take the risk of changing anyone's future. That means I'm keeping my own single status."

"Your sister happily changed Archie's future by agreeing to be his wife."

"Archie had already decreed he'd never join with another, and well before Marie had ever arrived. She changed nothing."

"You wish to live your life without ever knowing love?" He loosened the last lacing.

"No, but I'm out of choices." Bodice scrunched in her hands, she faced him. "Do you wish to marry one day?"

"Aye, I wish to wed, to find a wife who'll give me strong

sons and feisty daughters.”

“Have you ever courted a woman?” She toed off her silk slippers, nabbed her nightrail from her trunk and eased behind the silk dressing screen hand painted with a beautiful field of heather.

“Nay, and usually a man has to prove what he can offer when considering marriage, either by the strength of his sword arm, or by the lands he owns.”

“Do you have any land?” He certainly had a strong sword arm and she’d admired his fighting form often as he’d trained with his men. The man had muscles on top of muscles.

“A small parcel on Argyll adjacent to my brother’s. ’Twas land we received upon our father’s death. ’Tis no’ much, but there is a castle, even as rundown as it is.”

“Then why are you here and not there?” She shimmied out of her gown, tossed it over the top of the screen and donned her white cotton shift.

“The Isle of Islay is the land of my kin, and I’m still earning enough coin to effect adequate repairs on the castle. ’Twill be a beauty one day, solid and strong.”

“I’d love to see your land.”

“If you wish it, I will gladly take you. ’Tis but a short sail, except that any trip there would have to wait until the current threat from the MacLean clan eases.”

She walked out from behind the screen.

Lathering soap, John stood before the basin on the side table, his leather pants molding his tight butt and providing a delectable sight. He smeared bubbles along his jaw as he bent to the task.

Smiling, she crossed and lifted his shoulder-length brown locks wisped with blond. “My mother used to hold my father’s hair whenever he shaved. It saved getting suds in his hair. I’m not sure why, but he preferred the old hand razor over an electric shaver.”

"What's an electric shaver?" His golden gaze met hers in the looking glass propped before him.

"It's a device which plugs into a power source and when turned on, has sharp metal rotating heads that slice the stubble off at the root. No soap and blade is necessary."

"Is this the power source you called elec-tri-city?" He twisted his tongue around the foreign word she'd mentioned a few nights ago when she'd explained how energy was contained and dispersed, how electricity brought heat and light into a room and how it powered devices big and small. She'd boggled his mind when she'd spoken of email, letters that could be sent with the press of one button to anyone in the world.

"That's right."

"Do you miss the conveniences of your time? Many sound miraculous." He slid his dagger from ear to chin in one smooth move.

"Not yet, but I'm sure I will." She leaned into his back and covered his hand holding the blade. "Can I try that?"

He stopped, one brow raised. "You wish to shave me?"

"I saw a maid doing so for one of the warriors yesterday in the great hall. Is it not the right thing to ask?"

"The warrior you're speaking of is George. Three weeks past, he was hit by an arrow when Lachlan MacLean attacked Mary and Marie's party as they returned to Dunyvaig from the village of Ardbeg. The arrow embedded deep into his side and he cannae yet lift his arm. The maid shaves him so he willnae tear his stitches."

"Oh, I didn't realize."

He faced her, rested his backside on the table and extended his dagger toward her. "Shave me. I dinnae have an issue with it."

"Are you sure?"

"Aye, but take it slow." He pressed his dirk into her hands, cupped her hips and held her steady between his spread legs.

"I promise I'll do a good job." Turning his cheek with one finger, she held the blade nice and close to his skin and ran it in a smooth line down. "I'm also a quick learner, and if I make a mistake, I'll see it."

"My blood's red by the way." He squeezed her hips.

"So is mine." Grinning, she drew the dagger along the next portion under his chin and down his throat. "Goodness. It's like slicing through butter. I thought your stubble would be rougher to cut."

"I keep my dagger fastidiously sharp. Is that fire providing enough light?" His gaze darted toward it.

"Oh, no, you don't. I wouldn't move if I were you." She ran the blade right under his nose. "You wouldn't want me to nick this smart mouth of yours."

"I—"

"Don't speak either." She tapped his jaw shut and giggled. "This is so much fun. I never thought I'd ever get one-up on you." She shaved the bristles around his lips, not missing even one blade. "Mmm, that's smooth."

"Aye, there shall be no more whisker burn for the lasses after you're done."

"Then you can tell them to thank me." She slid the blade along the last stretch of his neck then dabbed his skin dry with the cloth. "Take a look in the glass. What do you think?"

He observed his reflection, patted his jawline and traced around his lips. "You've done a better job than I ever could have."

"Do you mind if I use your dagger to shave as well?" She wiped his blade clean on the cloth.

"Nay." His smile died away. "You're no' to take a blade to your soft skin."

"But my legs are itchy. I've never let them get so hairy."

"I said nay." He held out his hand for his dagger. "Women do no' shave their legs."

"They shave an awful lot more than that in my time." She passed it back, trod to her navy canopied bed and clambered under the covers. "I'll ask Mary for a blade in the morning."

"And I'll make sure she does no' give you one." He settled in his armchair, the pillow tucked behind his head.

"Then I'll pinch one from one of the warrior's when they're not watching."

"I'd like to see you try." He rolled his neck, scrunched his face then rubbed his nape as if in pain.

"John." She patted the space next to her and sighed. "Come and sleep beside me. I can't stand to see you so cramped and this bed is plenty big enough for both of us."

"Are you certain?"

"Yes, and the fact you're not saying no proves just how much you need to rest somewhere more comfortable than that chair. Please, it'll ease some of my guilt. It's my fault you feel indebted to remain."

"Aye, a fortnight in this chair has been long enough." He walked to the door, slid the bolt home then grabbed his pillow and ambled toward her. After sliding in under the covers, he stared at the wooden paneled ceiling above, a thoughtful look on his face. "I shouldnae ask, but where else does a woman shave? You've completely baffled me."

"I'll tell you, but only if you spill a secret about yourself as well." She snuggled into his side. The man exuded heat from every pore and the bed was cold. She may as well take advantage of the fact he could warm her quicker than anything else.

"Aye, that I can do." He wrapped one arm around her waist as he rolled onto his side and faced her. "Ladies first."

"Well, I've always preferred to remain bare below. I've waxed for years and I like feeling smooth, very smooth."

"Surely you cannae mean you wax your—" His gaze traveled down her body and he groaned.

"Yes, I wax down there."

"Oh hell. Clearly I shouldnae have asked." His cheeks flushed and she smiled.

"Waxing doesn't hurt, and I'm used to it although these days the candle wax I'm using takes a little more care and preparation compared to the modern day formula. Now it's your turn. Tell me your deepest, darkest secret."

"My secret isnae as personal as yours, but when I was a lad, I set out on an adventure. As I scaled Islay's cliffs, I discovered a hidden shaft covered by thick bushes."

"Oh, I love exploring. What did you find?"

"This particular shaft led to a sacred underground cavern. Except I couldnae wriggle through the last few feet to the interior, so instead I backed out and scoured the forest beyond the cliffs for another way in. That's when I discovered a tunnel winding deep into the earth. It came out afore a heavenly pool of crystal clear hot water."

"And you've never spoken of this to another?" She tucked a lock of his hair that had flopped forward, back behind his ear.

"I've no' told a soul, no' even Archie. This place is mine alone."

"Where is it, exactly?" There were cliffs all over Islay. It could be anywhere. "I'll never tell another soul either. I promise."

"'Tis no' far from here."

"Will you show me?" *Please say yes.*

"That might require us making another bargain." He picked up the amulet at her neck, closed his fingers around it and gently tugged her closer. "What do you wish to offer up for such a valuable piece of information?"

"The ultimate gift." She touched her nose to his and grinned. "I promise not to argue with you for one entire day."

Hmm, let him try not to take that bait.

* * * *

John chuckled as mischief danced in Katherine's big blue

eyes. She knew just how to tempt and entice him as no other woman ever had. "That is one tempting offer, little imp."

"I do try."

"I will need to think on it." He slid his fingers through her long white-blond hair glimmering gold in the firelight. "But mayhap from that chair. Being in the same bed as you is addling my senses."

"Nothing addles you." She traced the indent in his chin then kissed the spot. "Please, I'd love to see your sacred cavern."

"Mayhap if you spoke of your nightmares and shared the burden, I might consider that a justifiable bargain." He stroked down her sides and over her hips. "They haunt you and I cannae stand it."

"You strike a hard bargain." She breathed deep and slowly nodded. "All right. In my nightmares I see my death."

"What?" Surely she jested, only from the firm expression on her face, she didn't.

"When I'm asleep, I keep reliving the moment before I arrived, while I was stuck between times inside the faerie circle. I see myself bleeding from a wound on my neck." She nibbled on her lower lip and he rubbed his thumb along the reddened mark.

"Continue. I wish to hear it all."

"My dreams feel more like returning memories."

"You came through the veil with no wounds."

"Yes, which makes my dreams all the more strange." She trailed a finger down his neck and into the deep V of his tunic. "Do you recall Marie's neck wound?"

"Aye. When Archie took his blade to Lachlan during the battle at the Rhinns, Marie cried out and clasped her neck as a wound suddenly opened out of nowhere. Archie held his hand against MacLean, then bound hers and Lachlan's wounds. She bled because her paternal ancestor did."

"In my dreams, I suffered the same injury as Marie, in the

exact same spot."

"Archie didnae take MacLean's life. He bound her wound and she survived."

"There was so much blood, and I had no one there to stem the flow like Marie did."

"Nay, I dinnae believe it. You're alive and have no' perished." He pulled her closer, held her tight.

"I also dream of my parents. They were there with me in the circle and I have no idea how that could've happened, not when—" Tears pooled in her eyes. "I fought for each breath I could until one of the fae shimmered into sight and pressed again my chest. The heat of her touch moved through my body and everything felt so peaceful."

"I was there when you came through the veil." He aligned every inch of their bodies. "You were well and truly alive with no' a drop of blood on you."

"Yes, but I think the fae must have removed it. The next thing I remember is coming to and hearing Marie call my name. Then you and Archie arrived." She sniffed. "I know it all seems strange, but the moment you and I touched, I felt like I'd just come home, as if I was whole again."

"You are home when you're with me." Rubbing his cheek against hers, he gave into the deep need within him to draw her even closer. He rolled her onto her back and looked deep into her shimmering blue eyes. "Katherine, may I kiss you?"

Her breath hitched and her pupils darkened. "There's something about you that calls to me, but kissing really should be off the table."

"That's no' the answer I seek."

"If there's one thing I've learnt, history must remain on course." She raised a brow. "I can't change the path you're supposed to travel, and kissing me isn't part of that path."

"One kiss willnae change my future."

"You're also a temptation I need to resist."

"And you're a temptation I have no intention of resisting." He brushed his mouth over hers, so gently, so softly, then as she softened underneath him, he urged her lips farther apart and delved deeper into the delicious recesses of her mouth. Desire swarmed his senses and he feasted, kissing her as he'd secretly longed to since the moment they'd met.

"Oh my goodness, are we truly kissing?" She melted against him, her breath whispering softly across his tongue in a teasing caress he wanted more of.

"Aye, and I need another." He kissed her again, indulging and welcoming the raw intimacy he hadn't a chance of halting.

"You make me feel so alive, John." She tugged his shirttails free and slipped her hands underneath his tunic. Palms warm against his flesh, she stroked along his sides and over his lower back. "Tonight, the fae also told me there was magic all around me, and to draw on the touch of fae in my blood."

"You have fae in your blood?" He lifted up and stared into her eyes.

"Not that I've ever known. Neither of my parents certainly ever mentioned a thing." She pressed her breasts against his chest, kissed along his jaw and nibbled his ear. "You taste so good. Even though I shouldn't, I like kissing you."

"If you are part fae then that would explain how you so easily scatter my thoughts." He rubbed his hips against hers and his cock stiffened and pushed into her belly. "Aye, and far too much." He blew out a long breath and flopped onto his back. "My apologies. I've let things go too far."

"Don't be sorry."

"'Tis time for us to sleep." He fisted his hands so as not to reach for her again. "Rest, Katherine. I'll watch over you throughout the night."

"I know you will." She closed her eyes and as her breathing evened out, she fell asleep.

He too allowed sleep to take him.

Chapter 2

Content and deep asleep, images swirled through Katherine's mind. The lushness of the forest beckoned and John held her hand, his fingers tangled with hers as he led her along a thin leaf-strewn trail. Low branches brushed her arms as they tramped. "Where are we?"

"Close to the cliffs overlooking the ocean."

The sanctuary of the woods gave way to water gushing somewhere close by.

"We're almost there." He withdrew his sword and slashed the thick vegetation blocking the path then stepped through into a beam of sunshine.

She stumbled after him and gasped. Water rushed over a stone ledge, streamed around thick boulders and flowed into a river completely concealed and surrounded by towering trees. "What a beautiful waterfall."

"'Tis one that hides the entrance to my sacred cavern."

"I can't believe you actually brought me here."

"Destiny ensured 'twas so." He glanced skyward where thick gray clouds rolled in and blocked out the sun. "It looks like a storm is about to roll in. We need to hurry."

Birds twittered from their nests high above as he guided her toward the waterfall then jumped from boulder to boulder and onto the stone ledge. She followed in his tracks.

"This way." Between two cracks in the rock, slick with the water's spray, he squeezed through.

"I'm coming." She eased through the gap then scampered down the precariously wet tunnel carved of stone. "Thank you for sharing this place with me."

"You and I are bound, Katherine, in a way I dinnae understand. 'Tis best if there are no secrets between us." He leaped from the edge of the passageway and landed with a soft thump onto the grainy white sand three feet below. Arms extended, he nodded. "Jump."

She sprang into his arms and he swung her down beside him. Water lapped onto a small curved beach surrounded by black rocks glistening from the hot pool's rising steam. So beautiful.

"Do you see that vent?" He pointed upward at the craggy ceiling where a trickle of light beamed through a tiny cavity and washed over the pool's glassy, darkened surface.

"Yes. Is that the vent that leads out over the cliffs?"

"Aye, the very one, although 'tis too small to climb through."

"It's a wonder you ever found this place." She brushed gritty sand from her teal skirts and a stringy cobweb from her arm. "How often do you come?" It would be a crime not to enjoy the seclusion and beauty this place offered.

"There's rarely time when my duties to my clan come first." He removed his sword belt, propped it against a rock and divested himself of his wrist daggers. His dark brown hair wisped with golden ends swept his shoulders as he crouched at the water's edge and swirled a hand through. Waves rippled across the stillness.

"Sometimes one has to make time." Grinning, she unlaced her gown's front stays, wriggled her hips and allowed the fine velvet to slither to the ground. She picked it up, laid it overtop one of the boulders at the rear of the cave and rolled her sark's sleeves to her elbow.

"You shouldnae undress afore me in such a way." John stared at her, a hunger in his eyes that made her catch her breath, a look that she secretly loved.

"Sorry, but I don't see a dressing screen here." She dipped her toes into the water then waded in. Her ankle-length white linen shift tangled around her legs as she lowered to her chest. "In the future, women wear swimsuits, not a sark to swim in."

"And what is a swimsuit?" He perched on a rock and tugged off his boots.

"It's a small suit of clothing one wears in the water that allows fluid movement." She lifted her sark's hem over her head and tossed it onto the sand where it hit with a resounding slap.

John's hands stilled on the fastening of his white tunic's ties. He lifted his gaze and ogled the mop of wet linen on the sand. "You unclothed yourself?"

"I'm wearing the equivalent of a two-piece swimsuit underneath. My bra and panties will do as a bikini. A girl can't give up all her favorite pieces of clothing when she travels to the past. Anyway, it's dark and I'm underneath the water. Just strip off and hop in."

"You tempt me beyond my endurance." He shucked his tunic, leaving his black leather pants on as he strode toward her. His wide chest held a smattering of hair, the same dark shade as his head. Thick biceps bulged as he dove in, his entire body sculpted from hours of rigorous training. Underneath the water, he appeared as a murky shadow until he emerged in a spray of water, a mere breath before her. "Aye, 'tis dark enough. I see naught."

"Trust me. You've nothing to fear from my underwear. Let me show you." She caught his hands, slid them around her waist. "A bra has two pieces of fabric which cover a woman's breasts and—"

"Oh hell." He stretched his hands and spanned her bare skin more fully. "Your belly is exposed."

"And my legs." She eased his hands down her sides, over the thin silk edges of her pink panties and along her thighs. "But everything important is covered."

"'Tis becoming far too difficult to keep my hands off you." Husky words that made her shiver with need, and for the life of her, she couldn't push him away.

Instead, she rested her cheek on his chest and allowed the heavy beat of his heart to soothe her. For some reason, his life force did. "John, I—"

His form wavered and he disappeared.

Another barrage of images flared to life, of a scraggly bearded warrior with a grass-stained tattered tunic smeared with blood. The warrior hauled her toward a skiff beached on the shore of an isolated cove. "Make haste," the man snapped.

"You have to let me go." Arms bound behind her, she stumbled in her heavy sapphire skirts across jutting rocks and onto a pebbly beach, the sunshine glinting off her amulet and catching her in the eyes.

"The MacDonalds watch you like a hawk. The guards will notice you're missing afore too long. There can be no delay."

"Where are you taking me?"

"You're the faerie my chief brought into camp when we fought to take the Rhinns, the one who appeared from Dunyvaig's faerie stones. My chief believed since a MacLean came forth from the guardians' circle, it proves Islay belongs to us."

Few could tell the difference between her and Marie, and it could only have been her sister he'd spoken of. "I'm not only MacLean but also MacDonald."

"Aye, but with Lachlan choosing to use you to lure the MacDonalds into a battle, then so will I. Except on our own land where we'll have a greater fighting force."

"I'll never aid you in your war, not when the fae have given me the task to bring about some peace."

"There will never be peace." He spat on the ground. "You have the power to aid us in the return of our land, and even though the MacDonalds captured my chief and handed Lachlan over to the king's men following our battle, I willnae give up his fight. As my hostage, you'll provide me with the bargaining power I need over the MacDonalds. The Rhinns will be ours. Make no mistake about that." He tossed her into the skiff's hull, pushed the boat into the water and sprayed drops over her as he bounded in.

In the distance along the coastline, the MacDonald stronghold stood guard like a sentinel. She'd never wanted to leave John this way. Pain speared through her.

* * * *

A heart-wrenching cry echoed around the room and John snapped upright in bed.

"Please, no." Katherine sobbed as she stood across the chamber rocking before the narrow window, her face eerily pale in the moon's glow. "The MacDonalds will come after you, Finlay. There can be no more bloodshed."

"Katherine." He burst across the chamber, grasped her shoulders and turned her around. "'Tis I, John."

"So c-cold," she mumbled, her gaze blank.

"Wake and all will be well." He pulled her into his arms and murmured soothingly, "'Tis naught but a nightmare which holds you. Who's Finlay?"

"Finlay MacLean." She blinked and her gaze cleared. Clasping his face with chilled fingers, she gasped. "John?"

"Aye, you're awake now."

"I'm at Dunyvaig?" She glanced around the chamber, squeezed her eyes shut then opened them again. "My nightmares have taken a turn. I didn't dream of my death tonight but of something else."

"You spoke Finlay MacLean's name. Come and tell me all." He eased her in under the covers, wrapped himself around her in order to provide as much warmth as he could then nudged her to begin.

"The first dream was so sweet. You took me to your sacred cavern. A waterfall streamed over a stone ledge and a tunnel led deep underground. Steam rose and glistened over black rocks surrounding a pool of hot water."

"I spoke of the cavern this eve." Not that he'd mentioned the stone ledge and waterfall. "Mayhap you dreamt of it since 'twas one of the last things we spoke of."

"I saw it so clearly. A trickle of moonlight beamed in through an overhead vent that lead out over the ocean's cliffs. We swam and I listened to your heartbeat." She gripped his hem, lifted his tunic over his head and tossed it onto the floor. Swiftly, she edged over top of him and straddled his hips. Her gaze skimmed his chest then she wriggled down and pressed her ear to his chest. "The sound of your heartbeat soothed me, just as it soothes me now."

"Tell me more about the cavern." He couldn't deny the accuracy of her description of the hidden entrance.

"There was a hunger in your eyes and I wanted to kiss you." She pressed her mouth to his flat nipple, teased the tight flesh with her tongue and teeth and sighed. "Sooo good."

"Katherine, you cannae tempt me so." Sensations stormed through him, a whirlwind of desire and need. Nay, he wouldn't take advantage of her, not when she'd awoken so distressed. "You cried out and spoke of a MacLean warrior, that the MacDonalds would come for him, and that there can be no more bloodshed."

"One moment I was in the pool with you and in the next, the dream changed. I saw a warrior, a man who believed me to be Marie. He'd seen my sister during the battle at the Rhinns. I didn't deny I was her."

"We captured as many of the warriors who tried to take the Rhinns as we could. None remain on Islay, that I'm aware of."

"He was never caught but trekked here and now wishes retribution. He took me as his hostage, to use me as a bargaining chip in this war."

"I'd never allow the enemy to take you."

"The dreams feel so real, like a foretelling of things to come." She sat upright and planted her hands on his chest. "The faerie. She said there is magic all around me, that I only had to open my eyes to see it."

"Do you believe you have the sight?" He couldn't deny the extenuating circumstances of her arrival. Magic had brought her here, and through time itself. Perhaps her dreams were an omen of things to come.

"I've never seen the future unfold before, but then again, I've never traveled through time either. A lot of firsts have happened since I've arrived on your isle. I've dreamed of my parents, my own death, and now your cavern and my abduction. It all feels so real. I need answers."

"Mayhap it is all real." He caught her hands, pressed her palms to his lips and grazed his mouth across her soft skin.

"Oh, when you touch me like that, I swear I can feel it to the depths of my soul." She leaned in and brushed her lips across his. "Do you feel it too?"

"Aye." Since the moment she'd fallen through the veil something strong had bound them together. Deep in his soul, only peace came when she remained close by and within his sight. Cradling her face in his hands, he murmured, "On the morrow, I shall take you to my cavern. Promise me you'll keep its location a secret."

"Of course. I would never show another."

"Then 'twill be done." He wrapped his arms around her, held her close. "I'll permit no more secrets between us."

"You said that in my dream, or something very like it." She lifted her chin, her gaze firm on his.

"Then I clearly meant it. Rest now. I'll watch over you throughout the rest of the night."

"Thank you." She settled against him, her breath blowing warmly across his chest.

"Goodnight, my sweet imp. Your nightmares cannae continue forever. Together, we'll chase them away."

* * * *

A sliver of sunlight beamed through the wooden shutters over the narrow window and stirred John from his slumber. Katherine slept in his arms, her nose burrowed into his neck and her contentment bringing such peace to his soul. He stroked her back, so relieved her nightmares had not risen again to wake her.

"John?" Mumbling, she stretched and sighed.

"Shh, go back to sleep."

"Is it morning already?" She rubbed her eyes with her knuckles. "You usually have training at dawn."

"The sun has barely risen, and my men can wait a little longer."

"You never miss training." She wriggled higher, her long white-blond hair sliding over his chest, a silky touch that made him ache for more. "You shouldn't be staying for me."

"I'm in your bed and I dinnae care to leave it, no' yet."

A rap sounded. "My lady, 'tis Will. I search for John."

"He's here," she answered.

"Aye, Will, I'll be down shortly." He growled under his breath, detesting that he had to leave her so soon.

"Aye, Captain." Will's footsteps faded away.

"See, your men miss you when you're not where you should be."

"As I miss you when you're no' with me." He rolled Katherine onto her back, leaned over her and kissed the tip of her nose. "Since you spoke of your abduction last eve, it would pay for me to ensure an additional search of the woods is carried out this morn. I'll never allow a MacLean warrior to steal you away."

"I know you won't." She twined her arms around his neck, her fingers sliding deep into his hair.

Sharing her bed, having her open up about her nightmares, had changed something between them. She now touched him with more ease, and he adored it. "I willnae abide any possible threat to you or my clan. I need the description of the warrior from your dreams."

"They all feel so real."

"You accurately portrayed my cavern's entrance, a fact I cannae dismiss, and since you did so, you should also be able to do the same with the warrior and the location where he took you." Ever so gently, he trailed one finger across her high cheeks sprinkled with freckles and down along her lush lower lip. He longed to kiss her as deeply as he had last night, to feel the silky softness of her tongue licking across his, to take what she'd so willingly offered and allow that passion to consume them both. If only she weren't so damn adamant about not changing his future.

"You appear distracted, John." Those luscious lips lifted.

"Aye." He gave his head a shake to clear his thoughts. "A description if you please."

"He had brown hair, a scraggly beard, and green eyes." She wriggled free of him, crawled out of the covers and hopped off the end of the bed. "He also wore a grass and blood-stained tunic as if he'd been living on the run, but his weapons were in pristine condition, a sword and sheathed wrist and ankle daggers. My dream never showed where or how we met, just him dragging me toward an isolated cove. I recall looking from the skiff he'd tossed me in and seeing Dunyvaig on the cliffs, so the bay must be around two miles north of here. I can show you the location if you'd like. If I see it, I'll know it."

"Nay, you're to remain here where 'tis safe." He shoved the bedcovers aside, strode to the trunk under the window where he'd stored spare clothes and jerked on a white tunic. "That means you're to have a guard at your side at all times, and you're no' to wander from the tower watchman's sight until I've confirmed whether or no' a MacLean trespasses on our land." An increase in her protection was essential.

"I'm not used to being told where I can or cannot go. Women don't live under such restrictions in the future." She raised an eyebrow as if in challenge, a dare he was more than prepared to accept.

"You'll follow my orders or suffer the consequences." He nabbed his plaid, wrapped it around him then secured it with a silver pin across his chest.

"And those consequences would be…"

He slid his hand around her nape, backed her against the wall and pressed his entire length against hers. Damn it. He couldn't help but touch her. "The MacLeans are our greatest threat. Lachlan MacLean and Angus MacDonald are chiefs and brothers by marriage, but things have been so on edge between them for years. The chasm of hatred between the clans is too wide to mend, and whatever means the MacLeans have at hand to gain an advantage in this feud, they use. Certainly abducting you would be a loss I could never withstand."

"The fae have asked me to bring about peace."

"'Tis an impossible task and one I'll never condone."

"I'm here for a reason, whether you condone that or not." She slid one finger between his laces and traced over his heart. "If I'm to see to my mission, I need more knowledge on the MacLeans. Tell me how the feud began."

"You're no' aware?"

"Most of the history I've read has come from stories told down through the generations. I'd rather hear it directly from the source." She frowned, so adorably. "Please, don't make me go elsewhere for my information. I wish to hear how you believe this war has escalated to the point it's gotten to today."

"Mayhap if I explain the depth of it, and for how many years we've been plagued by the MacLeans then you might see just how futile the fae's request truly is."

"Maybe," she taunted. "Come on, John. What could it hurt to give me some more information?"

"Aye, I'll explain." 'Twould be best she learnt the details directly from him. "Five years past, Donald MacDonald sailed here to visit Angus. They're brothers and very close. But afore Donald and his men arrived, they were forced to take shelter on the Isle of Jura north of here as a storm passed through. That's when our troubles began. The northern half of Jura is held by Lachlan MacLean, but the southern half is Angus's. Donald landed on Lachlan's portion of the isle, yet thought himself on his brother's land. They made camp, and then in the dead of night while he and his men rested, they were viciously attacked by Lachlan and his warriors."

"For doing no more than seeking shelter?"

"It wasnae shelter Lachlan believed to be all they sought. Terreagh MacDonald, one of Donald's own men, had a grudge against Donald, and that night he used Donald's arrival on Lachlan's land to his advantage. He betrayed his chief, and to a MacLean no less."

"How did he betray him?"

"He carried off with some of Lachlan's cattle, then turned coat and informed Lachlan it had been Donald's doing. Lachlan's attack was swift. Lachlan and his warriors snuck into Donald's camp while his warriors slept. Sixty men lost their lives that night. 'Twas a terrible slaughter, one that can never be forgiven."

"A man's life is worth far more than a few stolen cattle. What a brutal feud." Tears welled in her eyes. "Although Donald clearly survived since he's now imprisoned in Edinburgh."

"Donald remained aboard his galley. He'd taken the sea watch so his men could get their rest. Sadly, he never saw the inland attack and had no knowledge of the battle until 'twas done."

"What happened next?"

"Angus heard about what had happened and visited Donald at Dunscaith Castle where he'd returned to lay his slain warriors to rest. Angus hoped to intervene, but Donald intended his revenge. So, to try to settle the issue, Angus detoured on his way home and paid a call on Lachlan at Duart Castle on Mull, hoping he could make his brother-in-law see reason. Lachlan though wouldnae be swayed, no' when things had always been so on edge between them. Instead Lachlan threw Angus into his dungeons then demanded he handover his lands in the Rhinns. Tensions exploded."

"The Rhinns is one place I'd love to explore. It's a wildlife sanctuary in the future and well protected." She slid her thumbs under his waistband, her fingers smoothing over his skin. "I think I understand Lachlan MacLean a little better."

"He's a warrior who'll use whatever unlawful means he can to get his way."

"Yet his clan admire and respect him." She tapped his chest. "He can't be all that bad."

"Of course they revere him. He fights for them, but never forget, he's a dangerous man."

"What about poor Mary? How did she cope when her own brother imprisoned her husband? She's never spoken of that time, and I've never asked."

"'She was distraught and suffered greatly. Even more so when she received a missive from Angus asking her to send their eldest son, James, to be held as Lachlan's hostage in Angus's stead. Sending her son away near broke her. The lad was only five at the time."

"Lachlan truly used an innocent child to gain what he

wanted?"

"Aye, and MacLean cared naught about the damage done to the lad. James was simply a means to an end." He stroked the back of her head in an attempt to sooth her clear distress. "After Angus's release, he asked Lachlan to meet him at Mullintrea near the Rhinns to sign the transfer parchments, and when Lachlan arrived with James at his side as leverage, Angus knew Lachlan would never hand his son over, no' even after the deed was signed and he'd received the Rhinns, so he came up with a plan. He demanded Lachlan settle their differences with honor and thankfully he agreed. Angus treated Lachlan well for the day, and once Lachlan and his men retired to the village for the night, Angus and his warriors surrounded their longhouse."

"And did more men die?" She squeezed her eyes shut and a tear trickled free. "How many perished this time?"

"When Angus finally had his brother-in-law cornered, Lachlan surrendered. Angus spared Lachlan's life that night so as not to escalate the feud, although he did take the life of Terreagh MacDonald who was amongst Lachlan's men. In the years since, Lachlan has continued to seek his revenge. He's ravaged our land where he could, and Angus has had no choice but to plunder in return. Angus's retaliation has been swift in order to ensure Lachlan cannae attempt to take it all once more." He cupped her face and gentled his tone. "Do you understand now why the fae's request to bring peace between the clans is impossible? There is no way to stem this feud. Lachlan is a tactical warrior, a man who fights to take it all. Even Mary's marriage to Angus has made no' a bit of difference, and she is his sister."

* * * *

"But I could still bring about some peace. Mary wants that too. She bestowed her amulet to my sister, so one day a child born of both clans would once again return to Islay. Now two have." Mary had held hope, and so would she.

"And what of your great desire no' to change history? Bringing about peace would achieve that very means when war continues to rage."

"I'm not going to alter the future, just provide some relief while keeping it on track. Why else would the fae have given me this mission?"

"I still cannae allow you to step one foot on MacLean land. There will never be peace." He caressed her sides, roamed down and scooped her bottom. Lifted higher, he pressed his hips against hers. "You'll do as I say and remain here where you'll be safe from any harm."

"You can't use your strength against me. I'm a twenty-first century woman, and we operate by a whole separate set of rules. Force isn't one of them." She seized his thick biceps and held on.

"I would never use force against you, no' by any means." He carried her to the bed and laid her across the mattress. Gently, he nudged her knees apart and with his legs between hers, sank down. He covered her mouth with his and kissed her, so sweetly she melted. He was so big and strong and all hers, or at least for this stolen moment in time.

"I love how you kiss me."

"And I love how you respond." With painstaking slowness, he grazed a finger along the upper swell of her breasts where her nightrail dipped. "I shouldnae be touching you so, but I cannae help myself."

"I ache, John, in places I've never ached before." She squeezed her eyes shut and when she opened them, she couldn't halt her plea. "Kiss me again."

He kissed her, a deep, devouring kiss that made her heartbeat flutter into a frenzy. "I give you my oath, Katherine. You will always have my protection, my absolute aid and undying loyalty. Dinnae you feel what's between us?"

"I do, and I want to take more just for myself, but changing the path your future is set on isn't right. Last night you told me of your desire to take a wife and to have children. I'll never be that person."

"You have too much love to give to withhold it."

"A stolen moment or two is all I can permit." She cupped his cheeks. "Although I have an admission if you wish to hear it."

"Speak it. No secrets are permitted between us."

"During the years of my mother's illness, both my sister and I spent all our time with her and never bothered delving into a relationship. In the future, women ensure their own protection, and I took care of that in case I ever needed it in place. I can't fall pregnant, or at least not for the next two months. The precautions I took are ninety-nine percent effective. I had an injection"—she tapped her arm—"right here."

He frowned and smoothed his fingers over her arm. "I dinnae see how your arm can protect you against what goes on far below."

"There are incredible medical advances in my time that provide the protection I'm talking about. Believe me, I'm protected."

"What are you trying to say?"

"That an affair between us is possible, provided it's a short one."

"An affair isnae what I'm after." He lifted himself up, gripped her hands and tugged her to her feet. With a scowl, he picked up his sword and belt. "I have duties to attend to."

"You're angry that I've asked for an affair?"

"You deserve more than just a toss of your skirts and a hard and fast tumble." He strode to the door and eyed her. "I'll send a maid with your bath and a tray then return for you at the midday meal. Be prepared for a swim."

"I'll be ready."

He closed the door and her heart grew heavier as his footfalls trailed away. From the moment she'd fallen through the veil and into his arms, their connection had fused and only deepened in the weeks that had followed. Opening up to him last night about her nightmares had been inevitable, her trust in him absolute. She'd not even spoken of them to Marie, her own sister who she never kept a secret from.

At the hearth, she clasped the rod and prodded the embers. The ashes glowed red and she added shaved bark and wood chips as John usually did each morning to ensure the fire blazed as she bathed. The flames flickered and she laid a block of peat on top, brushed her hands and stood.

At a knock on the door, she crossed and bid two lads to enter. Barefoot and with sooty imprints on the knees of their loose-legged breeches, they heaved a tub before the fireplace then scurried out. A servant entered carrying a tray with a steaming bowl of oats and a trencher of meat. The maid set it on the side table then took the water basin John had used to shave with last night and tossed the soapy mess out the chamber window.

Another maid arrived, placed a drying cloth and bar of soap next to the water jug and set a clean basin down while another lass crossed to the navy curtained ambry with an armful of clothing. As she laid the clothing on the bed, a splash of teal peeked through from underneath a fur cloak.

"What do you wish to wear, my lady?" The maid hung the garments.

"The teal gown. Leave it out, please." It was the gown she'd dreamed she'd worn to the cave and it seemed right to ensure she donned it today.

The maid directed the lads as they returned with pails of steaming water, then she added vanilla scented oil and a sprinkle of dried petals. Done, she closed the door behind her after the servants filed out.

Alone, Katherine sat at the side table, lifted the small bowl of honey and swirled it over top of the hot oats. She slid a spoonful into her mouth. Delicious, and it tasted exactly like Mum used to make on those cold winter mornings when she'd been a child. Her chest throbbed and she blinked furiously, suddenly fighting tears. Grief hit at the most unexpected times, when a thought or memory fluttered. She and Marie talked often about Mum, but her sister wasn't here to share her current burden. Her mother's passing at forty-five had been far too young, but cancer struck no matter what age. At least they'd had three years together before her illness had finally taken her.

Scrubbing a hand over her face, she murmured, "I miss you Mum. I wish you could have lived and traveled to this glorious place."

The wind whistled through the window the maid had left partially open and lifted her hair across her face. Soft words whispered through. "I am always with you."

"Who is that?" She spun about then hurried to the window and planted her hands on the stone windowsill. Thick tree branches scraped against the side of the castle and birds twittered from within the thick green foliage, but not a soul was in sight. She opened the window wider and sunshine beamed in, hit the looking glass and sent prisms of colors shimmering all around her.

"You're alive and well, my daughter." More whispered words, but coming from where?

"Mum?" She searched the chamber but saw nothing. "Are you really here?"

"Yes, but I can't draw together a form you can see unless there are enough elements in the air to do so. The last time we spoke, I managed it by bringing forth mist and moonlight."

"I can't believe you're here." She grasped her chest and tried to breathe through the pounding of her heartbeat. "Does that mean all my dreams are real?"

"Yes, and I'm here now because you need me. Death came but couldn't take you, not when you and I both begged the fae to intervene. To ensure your survival the fae bound you to another here in the past, the warrior, John MacDonald. You must keep him close as the fae instructed you to."

"I know I'm supposed to keep him close, but bound? What do you mean by bound?"

"As you drew your last breath, a piece of your soul lifted free and bound itself to him. You cannot live if he doesn't."

"Holy moly." That she'd never seen in her dreams, yet she couldn't deny the depth of their bond. She thrived on being close to him, but why would the fae do that? "Mum, his future is set. He's meant for another."

"Your soul would not have been bound to his if that were so." Her mother's voice drifted to the area behind the looking glass propped on the side table.

Katherine stepped up to the glass and gasped at her own reflection. Her white-blond hair shimmered and her skin sparkled. Blue eyes, a midnight shade, twinkled as bright as precious sapphires. She patted her flushed cheeks. "What's happening to me?"

"Your fae blood strengthens now you're in this time and closer to the fae realm. Embrace that part of you and allow the visions you've had to guide you. They will come when they're needed, and only then." Warm air swished around and soothed her. "You must accept your place here in the past as Marie has done. You and your sister are two halves of one whole, the beginning and the end, and I wish for you the life you should always have—"

The door banged open and John stood there, his chest heaving, his gaze moving frantically around the room then over her. "Why are you glowing?"

"My mother is here. Why are you back?"

"Because my chest aches and I can feel your distress as if it were my own." He closed the door and grasped her hand. "Where is she? Your mother?"

"I can't stay, Katherine," her mother whispered, "and only you can hear me. Blood of my blood and no other. Stay safe. As the fae said, '*To bring peace, you must unite.*'" Her voice floated away, and as the sun slipped behind a layer of cloud, the room darkened. In the looking glass, the glow around her dispersed and she once again appeared her usual self.

"She's gone, but she was here. My mother came to me, as I dreamt she did in the circle. It's all real. All of it."

"I believe you." He gripped her shoulders, ran his hands down her arms and back up again as he stared into her eyes. "You feel far too warm."

"My mother told me my fae blood strengthens now I'm in this time and closer to the fae realm. I'm to embrace that part of me and allow my visions to guide me. We're soul bound."

"What? Soul bound? Are you sure? How did that happen?"

"In the circle, I breathed my last and the fae intervened. A piece of my soul lifted free and bound itself to you. It's you who keeps me grounded to this time." Her fingers tingled and she clenched and unclenched her fists. "I cannot live if you do not. My mother's words, and they were crystal clear."

He lifted her hands to his lips, ran his thumbs across her palms then blew cool air across them. "What I feel for you runs deep and has since the moment we met. In truth, I can easily accept we're soul bound. I freely desire such a bond."

"Being soul bound doesn't mean I'm going to change your future. It just means I have to take more care."

He tipped up her chin with one hand, wrapped his arm around her waist with the other and drew her more fully against him. Every inch where they touched sizzled. Even her nipples ached, so sharp and painfully.

"The more we're together, John, the closer we become."

"Aye."

"We can't allow this bond to take us over." She pulled away and paced the chamber. "We'll need a plan."

"Katherine." John stepped in her path and blocked her way. "I dinnae care to see you so anxious."

"Everything's changed."

"Aye, but in a good way."

"In a way that can never last."

"I willnae take things further with you unless you wish it. I give you my word on that. I'm no rogue."

"I need some time to think through all that my mother has said."

"Then take that time, but this afternoon, we will talk more." He dropped a kiss on the top of her head and left, his last glance over his shoulder, a smoldering one.

The heat in his golden gaze spoke of promises she longed to accept, to claim for herself. If only she'd always lived in this time. No matter what her mother said, his future was set.

Chapter 3

Katherine shed her nightrail and stepped into the tub. After sinking into the glorious water, she lazed her head on the rim and relaxed with a heartfelt sigh. She needed this moment, to consider all her options. Traveling to her MacLean kin on Mull and seeing to the fae's request was paramount. The mission given to her by the little folk had to come first.

She stroked the amulet at her neck. Mary's talisman, now hers to hold, would provide the safe passage she needed. Only how could she change John's mind about coming with her?

The water cooled and she picked up the soap and lathered it. She went under then emerged and worked soap bubbles through her hair. Done, she dipped and rinsed again

"Katherine?" A knock sounded on the door. "'Tis Mary. John sent me to sit with you. He worries."

"Come in, Mary."

Mary bustled in wearing a billowy burgundy gown, her riot of red-gold curls swaying forward over her distended belly, her baby now due in only a few more weeks. Slowly, she eased into the navy padded corner armchair, stretched her legs and wriggled her slippered feet. "So, what have you done to cause poor John to worry this day?"

"He worries because last night I was drawn to the circle and once I slipped inside, one of the fae spoke to me." Leaning closer to Mary, she rested her arms on the rim. "I've been instructed to wear your amulet and to journey to Mull. Apparently I'm to bring some peace between the clans."

"Oh, I see." A frown marred her brow. "Then 'tis no wonder he worries. So many times I've stood inside the circle and wished for peace between my clans. The war that rages breaks my heart, and now you and Marie are here at a time when things are so unstable." She rubbed her belly then rose to her feet. "The babe kicks up a storm this morn. 'Tis difficult to sit still for long."

"Would going for a walk help to ease your discomfort?"

"Aye. Some fresh air and movement would help." Massaging her back, Mary waddled back and forth across the room.

"Give me a minute to get dressed and we'll go for a walk together." She set the soap aside as she stepped out of the water then grabbed the drying cloth and patted herself dry.

"When I left John below in the great hall, he was busy rousing a party of warriors to search the woods. He insisted every inch be scoured for MacLeans. Do you know what that might be about?"

"I take it you asked him but he didn't wish to worry you?" She donned her pink silk bra and panties, a sark, then eased the teal gown over her head. The soft folds shimmered down her hips and swished to her ankles. She laced the front stays to the top of the square-cut neckline trimmed with a lacy ribbon, then slid her feet into the matching slippers.

"Aye, he's a stubborn lout, as are all men."

She laughed as she picked up a brush, separated her hair into sections and combed. "Oh Mary, we are kindred spirits. I couldn't agree more."

"Mount up and prepare to leave." John's order rumbled

through the open window.

Katherine hurried across. Below in the courtyard, twenty or so MacDonald warriors mounted their horses while an equal number wearing green, red and blue plaids raced under the arch and down the trail to the sea-gate. John led the group heading toward the birlinn moored at the stone landing while a redheaded lad ran to keep up with his fast stride. James. Mary's eldest son was only ten yet was always in the thick of things

John leaped on board and offered James a steadying hand as he bounded in after him.

Mary peered over Katherine's shoulder. "Since John is taking my son with him, his mission cannae be too dangerous."

"He's only looking for one man, so no, it shouldn't be."

Mary squeezed her arm. "Please tell me what this is all about, or I shall go mad with wonder."

"Last night I had a dream, or I should say a vision. A MacLean warrior by the name of Finlay abducted me. Now John has decided to take every precaution and search for him."

"I know of a MacLean warrior named Finlay. He was often assigned to watch-point duty. The man had eagle eyes and could move like a shadow. Since one of Lachlan's greatest battle strategies is to keep a close eye on his enemy, I've no doubt one or two of his warriors continue to remain on Islay even though they lost the battle at the Rhinns."

"All to oars and ready the sail." John strode to the helm, a commanding presence with his brown and blond streaked hair brushing his claymore strapped in a baldric across his back. He appeared every inch a warrior prepared to battle. Pumping a fist in the air, he shouted, "We search for MacLeans and will remove any threat against our clan."

The men rowed then as the sail caught the fresh breeze, the birlinn sped out of the bay and beyond her sight toward the north. In the courtyard, dust plumed as the strong contingency of mounted warriors galloped out the gate and rode into the forest.

"You'll need to take great care if you're experiencing such visions, Katherine." Mary breathed deep. "You must no' speak of them around any other than those you hold absolute trust with. These are dangerous days for any who might be called out as a witch. The stake is no place for you."

"I'll be careful, very careful. Let's go for that walk." She looped her arm through Mary's and guided her out the door.

"Moving certainly eases the pain and the midwife will have me abed for a sennight or more once the babe is born. I long to feel the sunshine on my face afore the opportunity passes me by."

"Then sunshine you'll get." She wandered with Mary down the winding stairwell and into the great hall where beautiful tapestries hung on the stone walls. Above the blazing fireplace, a massive two-handed great sword encrusted with precious stones, glinted. She rounded the trestle tables and ambled past a maid wiping the elevated dais's tabletop. Near the door, a boy wearing tan breeches two inches too short and a long green tunic, swept dust into a pile.

They eased past him, walked outside and crossed the stony courtyard where a cart had been loaded with supplies and tools to complete the rebuild at Ardbeg. Following an attack by the MacLeans a few short weeks ago, fires had raged and destroyed a number of longhouses within the seaside village. A score of warriors left each day to join the villagers and aid them in repairing their homes.

They continued on, through the arched gates then down the steep trail to the lower courtyard. Along the pebbly beach, white-capped waves tumbled in and retreated leaving dense foam and tangled seaweed.

A guard followed them then halted a short distance away, ensuring their protection even as he allowed them a little privacy. He scanned the forest's tree line, his gaze on the constant move.

Katherine couldn't help but shake her head. "I hate that we all have to live so on guard."

"Aye, but this is lovely, being outside. 'Tis just what I needed." Mary waddled across to a boulder and perched on top of it, her burgundy skirts skimming the stones around her. She surveyed the bay and smiled as two fishermen rowed their skiff in and hauled it half onto the beach. They knelt before flat stones and cleaned their catch as a maid with her hair hidden underneath a frilly white linen cap dashed down from the castle with a wooden pail and set it next to the men.

Katherine sat on the boulder next to Mary. "I need you to tell me more about Lachlan. John enlightened me this morning about how the feud began, but I feel as if there's more to it."

"Of course, if it shall aid you. Lachlan was my father's only son, his heir and successor." She clasped her hands in her lap. "My sisters and I adored him, although Lachlan grew up well afore his time since Father passed when he was only fifteen. He was still a minor when he had to lead our clan. Even so, we called him Big Lachlan. Fifteen he may have been, but no one could miss him in a crowd, no' when he towered over them all. His skills were immense, and he excelled with the sword. He also learnt at a young age that if he wished to hold his position then he needed to fight. He battled, for land, for his kin, and for all that he desired." She rolled her shoulders and stretched her back. "As such, little ever escaped Lachlan's notice. He's a strategist, as my father never was."

"Your father died young, didn't he?"

"Aye, and he enjoyed his pleasures and burdened our clan with large debts in his five years as chief. Now Lachlan wars as he does in order to return to our clan all Father lost."

A seagull squawked as it circled overhead. It followed the maid as she clomped back uphill toward the castle, her full pail scraping the odd bump in the winding track.

She rose and edged in behind Mary. "Children in this day

grow up far faster than they should, but to lead an entire clan at fifteen is quite an accomplishment." With one knee resting on the boulder, she bent and massaged Mary's lower back. "Tell me if this helps or hurts."

She sighed with delight. "Ahh, 'tis wonderful, and aye, Lachlan's ability to lead is strong. I worry though. There's no telling what he'll do once presented with the king's demands."

"King James VI was known as one of the greatest kings of all times." What she'd read about him in the future had intrigued her. Because of his birth, he'd successfully united the kingdoms of England and Scotland at the turn of the coming century. He'd led with determination during his long reign. "I wish I'd tried to read up more about this feud. What of Lachlan's family on Mull? How do you think they'll fare with him being imprisoned?"

"Lachlan wed Lady Margaret, the Earl of Glencairn's daughter afore our feud began. They have bairns, and she's a caring woman. Five years ago when I was forced to send James to Duart as a hostage in my husband's stead, she did all she could to ensure my son didnae suffer too greatly. Even though I wasnae there, James told me so himself." She wriggled higher and tapped her sides. "Here too, please. The pain stretches wide."

"John mentioned that to me, that James was brought into this feud. I'm so sorry that happened to your son."

"'Tis our captain, Archie MacDonald," a guardsman shouted as he rushed across the top of the barbican. "He returns."

"Archie and Marie are back?" Excitement thrummed through her. With her hand on her brow, she searched the coastline toward the south. "I don't see anyone."

"Aye, look." Mary pushed to her feet. "There beyond the whitecaps. Archie's already lowered the sail."

A large wave rolled in and Archie's skiff came into sight. He gripped the boat's rudder, adjusted his course toward the sea-gate and cruised in.

One of the guards jumped into the waist-high water, seized the bow and roped the skiff to a catch between two bobbing birlinns.

In black pants and a white tunic fluttering free, Archie bounded onto the landing. He extended a hand to Marie and she grinned and leapt into his arms, her long white-blond hair streaming behind her in the brisk sea breeze. Her sister wore a pair of borrowed lad's breeches and a matching beige colored shirt that had to be Archie's since it enveloped her to her knees. Marie still struggled with the long gowns and wore pants whenever it suited, and going sailing definitely suited.

Archie adjusted a travel pack over his shoulder and with his arm around Marie's waist, guided her over the slippery stones and onto the grassy verge. Her sister's rosy cheeks and wide smile gave evidence of her happiness. She couldn't be happier for her. Marie had fallen in love with a man who would protect her with his last breath.

"Marie!" She waved out and her sister spun around, waved back then raced toward her. Arms opened, she caught Marie as she plowed into her. "Whoa."

"I missed you, sis." Marie bounced around in a little circle.

"I've missed you more." She breathed in her sister's sweet white rose scent and squeezed her tight. "Tell me everything you got up to on your honeymoon, and don't miss out on one thing."

"Archie kept me naked most of the time." Marie chuckled. "But I don't think that's what you meant. One sec." She reached out and pulled Mary into their hug. "I've missed you too, Mary. How's the baby?"

"The babe kicks something fierce this day." Mary kissed Marie's cheek. "I shall go and welcome Archie home and allow you two to catch up."

"Be careful walking across the beach." She squeezed Mary again then let her go. "I'll hunt you down later so we can chat."

"I'll look forward to it." Mary toddled off toward Archie

now surrounded by warriors clapping him on the back.

Marie clasped Katherine's face and touched their foreheads together. "I loved my honeymoon, but I feel like I left you behind to fend for yourself. Has John looked after you? What about your nightmares? Have they eased at all? You're all I could think about while I was gone."

"I better not have been, and yes, John watches over me, like a hawk. There's so much I have to tell you, but you go first. I want to hear all about the Rhinns. Is it as beautiful as everyone says?"

"It's stunning, and I can see exactly why Lachlan MacLean battles for it. It's such a large parcel of land with lochs and bens and grassy moors. We made camp along the beach when we first arrived, tramped and explored the reserve. It's the perfect sanctuary for wildlife. You and I have to go there together, and soon, before autumn passes. The golden-bronze colors of the trees, and the thickness and beauty of the forest reminds me of the Gold Coast's National Park. You remember that camping trip Mum took us on to the Park when we were fifteen, right?"

"I'll never forget it." Sweet memories stirred. The day they'd arrived at the park, Mum had popped the trunk, heaved out the tent and tipped it from its bag then stared at it in horror as she realized she'd left the setup instructions at home on the kitchen bench. So many poles, cords, and yards of canvas had spilled out, a jigsaw of pieces that had taken them hours and hours to sort through and put together. "Dad couldn't make that trip and it was just us three girls."

"We had the best time though." Marie sat on the boulder Mary had vacated and tugged her down beside her. "Now it's your turn. Tell me what you've been up to."

"Well, I don't quite know where to start."

"At the beginning."

"I spoke to Mum."

"What?" Her sister's eyebrows soared into her hairline.

"You just can't blurt something like that out. Are you serious?"

"Deadly serious. It appears time travel and visits from those in another realm are both entirely possible." She heaved in a deep breath. Now her sister was back, it was time to confess the depth and truth behind her nightmares.

"Come on, spill. You can't leave me dangling." Marie gripped her hands. "We've never kept anything from each other, and we're not starting now. What do you mean by you spoke to Mum?"

"I heard her voice and felt her presence, both while I was in the circle before I traveled here, and then again this morning, although I didn't recall her presence in the circle at the time. It appears my nightmares have in fact been returning memories."

"Start with when you were in the circle." Marie jiggled her legs, clearly anxious to hear all.

"When I was waiting for you to complete your mission, I collapsed and bled from a wound on my neck that opened out of nowhere. As you suffered during the battle at the Rhinns, so did I, but in the future, or perhaps somewhere in between realms. Mum told me this morning that death came but couldn't take me, not when the fae intervened. To ensure my survival the fae bound me to another here in the past and healed my wound. I must have been unconscious for parts of it since I only recall bits and pieces even now."

"Who did the fae bind you to?"

"John. He now holds a piece of my soul and the fae have said I must keep him close. I cannot live if he doesn't."

"Oh my goodness." She clutched her chest, her face paling.

"No, it'll be all right. I'm certain of that." She pulled Marie into her arms. "I'm alive now and here with you. That's all that matters."

"What else did Mum have to say?"

"That we hold fae in our blood and now we're in this time and closer to the fae realm, it's strengthened. Last night, I had two new visions and she told me to embrace and allow them to guide me. Dad's with her, sis." She touched the amulet at her neck. "Last night, the fae gave me a mission. I'm to wear Mary's talisman so it will provide me with safe passage as I return to our MacLean kin on Mull. I'm to bring peace between the clans."

"That doesn't make sense." Her frown deepened. "Peace doesn't come for some years and we're supposed to be keeping history on course, not changing it. Are you sure that's what you were told to do?"

"Yes. I haven't mistaken the fae's words, but maybe I'll get more clarity on my mission once I arrive on Mull. John actually said the same as you."

"Where's John now since you're supposed to be keeping him close?" Marie studied the warriors surrounding Archie.

"He sailed out earlier this morning. Last night during one of my dreams, I had a vision of a warrior abducting me from a bay a few miles north of here. John's gone in search of him, and to remove the threat."

Farther down the beach, Archie left his men and strode toward them, his brown hair wisped with blond, brushing his broad shoulders. Although not identical, he and John both shared similar physical features and the same towering height.

He halted before her and crossed his arms. "My men just informed me of the threat against you, Katherine."

"John's dealing with it."

"As he should, but you two are sitting out here when it will be far safer if you're both behind Dunyvaig's walls. John would insist on it, and so do I."

"I doubt any MacLean warrior will get through you or your guards, no matter where we sat." A fact he couldn't dispute.

"Aye, but a storm brews and I cannae protect you from its fury out here."

"What storm?" Only a peek of gray cloud sat on the far horizon.

"The weather can change in an instant in the isles." Archie motioned out to sea. "The waves grow higher and foamier and do you no' feel the heaviness in the air?"

"If Archie says a storm's on its way, there's one on the way, sis. Let's go inside." Marie's belly gurgled and she laughed and rubbed it. "I'm also starving. Archie insisted we set sail at dawn and I didn't get the chance to eat breakfast."

"I would have fed you, but we ran out of time when you had other ideas than breaking your fast in mind." Archie's golden eyes glimmered as he extended his hand toward Marie and tugged her to her feet. "Come. The midday meal now awaits."

"Great." Marie reached back for her, nabbed her hand and hauled her up too. "Come on. I really am hungry."

Teal skirts lifted, she walked beside Marie up the grassy rise as Archie kept guard at their back. A tingle of unease chased up her spine. John had promised to return by midday and though he only sought one man, she was suddenly anxious. Squeezing her sister's arm, she said, "If you don't mind, I might just see if I can spot John's birlinn from the battlements. I'll be inside soon."

"That's fine with me." She glanced at Archie. "Is that okay with you?"

"Aye, that willnae be a problem." He nodded then motioned the tower guard to lower the portcullis. The clunky sound of its chains reverberated throughout the keep as the metal grate lowered from within the stone-arched entrance gate.

"Make sure you come inside before it rains." Marie slipped her arm through Archie's and cuddled into his side as she walked into the keep.

Katherine trotted up the stairs to the battlements and gripped the thick stone crenellation. Past the bluff, the northern waterways remained clear. No birlinn and no John, or at least that she could see. The headland would provide an even better view.

A cool breeze blew over her and she shivered as the distant gray clouds thickened and covered the skies. If she wanted to get to the bluff, she'd have to sneak out since Archie had now secured the castle.

Hustling, she headed downstairs and skirted the curtain wall. The sentry guard paced the ramparts above and as he marched in the opposite direction, she snuck through the postern gate.

Into the forest, she dashed then followed the thin winding path to the headland. The wind whistled through and the autumn leaves lining the trail swirled in a whirlpool of russet and burnt orange at her feet.

Breathing hard, she finally stumbled onto the craggy bluff's cliff-top point. The bay she'd been taken from should be just visible, yet still there was no sign of John's birlinn. "Where are you?" she whispered into the wind.

Thunder boomed and the sea crashed hard against the jagged rock wall. Spray flew and drenched her. She slipped, made a grab for the cliff but only managed air. Screaming, she plunged toward the sea and hit the frigid water. Down she went, her breath lost at the hard impact. Her skirts dragged and the murky waves tossed her about. So deep.

What had she been thinking to stand so close to the edge? Goodness. She shouldn't have left the castle without a guard. John would certainly be furious to hear she'd snuck out. Kicking, she strived to get to the surface.

Her back slammed into the cliff and black hazed her vision. She shoved the dark away, seized the cliff's edge and held on with her life as the waves pounded into her from behind. No giving up. Along the rock face, several grooves appeared deep enough to use to pull herself up. Death wouldn't take her, not again, not when she had everything to live for. All she had to do was scale this cliff and reach the top. Then sneak back into Dunyvaig before anyone realized what she'd done. Totally doable. Or it better damn well be doable. She didn't want to consider the trouble she'd be in if John discovered what had happened.

Grunting, she heaved upward, intent on using whatever crack or ridge the rock offered. Determination spurred her on and as she passed the halfway mark, she clambered onto a thin ledge twenty feet from the top. Breathing hard, she flopped onto her back.

Above, the storm clouds continued to bubble and brew, whipping into a frenzy of vicious black. With frozen fingers and shaky legs, she gathered what strength she had and patted the rock above her head where a scraggly clump of bushes protruded from a crevice. Her hand sank through the brush and into a dark hole. Gasping, she scraped dirt and grit from around the edge and discovered a thin shaft leading inward. It appeared too small for her to fit into, unless she could scrape more of the dirt—

"Katherine!" At John's fierce shout she almost fell off her precarious perch.

Below, he stood at the bow as he cruised toward her, savage fury etched on his face.

"Wait right there!" He tore off his belted plaid, tossed it to one of his men then sprang into the raging waters, boots and all.

Oh great. So much for sneaking back in.

Chapter 4

Katherine clung to the ledge as John powered through the stormy waves toward her. He grasped the rock face and hauled himself up the cliff. Water sluiced down his body, plastered his white tunic to his chest and molded his black leather pants to his legs. The man looked incredible even though a fierce scowl darkened his face.

Swiftly, he climbed then clambered onto her ledge and crouched, his gaze moving over her. "What the hell do you think you're doing on this cliff? And where the hell is your guard?"

"I—I—" She shivered from head to foot, so cold from her dunking. "I needed to know where you were. I'm sorry. I never intended to fall but only to keep a lookout from the cliff top."

He shot a look upward then back down at the raging sea. Eyes wide, he bit out, "You fell? From the top?"

"Yes, and I was just making my way back up again when you found me."

"I'll kill whoever let you pass through the gates alone."

"This is no one's fault but my own. I snuck out the postern gate after Archie had secured the keep." She motioned toward the vent she'd found. "There's a shaft here, although it's too small to wriggle through and I don't know where it leads. The only way out, appears to be up."

"Aye, I know of this vent. I found it when I was a lad."

"How did you—hold on." Was it possible this was the shaft that led to his sacred cavern? "You said you were scaling Islay's cliffs when you discovered the underground cave? There's no way to scale this cliff, unless you too fell from the top."

"Aye, I recall the fall well." He snaked one arm around her waist, lifted her to her feet and pinned her to the cliff with his body. To his men below, he yelled, "Once we reach the top, sail for Dunyvaig. We'll return as soon as we're able." In her ear, he rasped, "I'll give you a boost. There are enough ridges in the cliff to climb the rest of the way to the top. Take it slow and tread with care. I'll be here, one step behind you."

"And to think you just told me off for falling from this cliff when you did the same exact thing. Unbelievable."

"Go, now, afore my heart leaps right out of my chest." He popped a kiss on her brow. "I cannae stand to see you clinging to this wall."

"You be careful too. It's slippery, and the water's rather cold. I don't recommend another dunking." She sucked in a deep breath and forced herself to move. Heaving upward, she clambered from one hand and foot-hold to the next.

John, like a shadow, trailed in her wake, his hand cupping her heel when needed and ensuring her footing remained firm.

After climbing past the scraggly bushes, she scrambled over the top and rolled onto the flat hard rock. On her back, she shoved clinging strands of wet hair from her face. "John?"

"I'm here." With one hearty heave, he tumbled in beside her and pulled her into his arms. "You shall never leave the castle again without a guard. I want your word on that, Katherine."

She pushed up onto one elbow and looked into his eyes. "Thank you for helping me."

"Give. Me. Your. Word."

The clouds opened and the rain beat down. Even though she was a wet, shabby mess, she smiled. "This isn't how we were supposed to arrive at the cavern. You took me by way of the forest entrance, and in my dream the rain clouds loomed but hadn't broken. This is all kinds of wrong."

"What are you saying?"

"Your day was planned until I told you about my kidnapping. You were supposed to train with your men, return for the midday meal and then bring me here. I've changed the events of the future by telling you, and I shouldn't have." She wiped the rain streaming down her cheeks with her gown's wet sleeve.

"You cannae expect each and every day to be as it should. There will be a variance simply because you are here."

"The variance is greater because I spoke about my vision."

Birds soared above then dipped and landed on the highest branches of the towering trees at the forest's edge.

Fingers numb and chilled, she clasped the amulet swinging at her neck. "This has been a lesson well learned, that it'd pay for me not to speak of my future visions with you."

"Nay, you will keep naught from me. I'll never allow it." He rolled her onto her back, and shielding her from the brunt of the pelting rain, narrowed his gaze. "I didnae find the MacLean warrior, nor even any sign of the skiff he uses to steal you away in. I need your word you'll remain at Dunyvaig until he's found. I've no wish to lock you in your chamber and bolt your door."

"I won't change the future now I'm aware of the d-dangers that l-lurk." Teeth chattering, she cupped his cheeks. "I'm c-cold, really cold. Can we get out of here?"

"Aye, the cavern is close. We'll stop and warm up afore we trek home." He rose, slid his hands around her waist and set her on her feet.

She burrowed against his side and together they hurried into the woods until the darkness of the forest closed in around them.

They tramped along a sodden trail then slowed as water gushed somewhere close by. "Is that the river?"

"The very one." He withdrew his sword and slashed the thick vegetation blocking the thin leaf-strewn path before stepping through.

She stumbled after him and gasped. Water rushed over a stone ledge, streamed around thick boulders and flowed into a river completely concealed and surrounded by towering trees. "It's all exactly as I saw it."

"Let's hurry. The storm worsens." He glanced to the heavens where lightning slashed the sky in a frenzy of electric whites and yellows. With his hand at her back, he guided her toward the stone ledge. Between two cracks in the rock, slick with the water's spray, he squeezed through.

She wriggled inside after him and scampered down the precariously wet tunnel carved of stone. "Thank you for sharing this place with me."

"You and I are bound, Katherine. I'll permit no secrets between us, a fact you will learn swiftly and well." He leaped from the edge of the passageway and landed with a soft thump on the grainy white sand three feet below. Arms extended, he nodded. "Jump."

She sprang into his arms and he swung her down beside him. Water lapped onto a small curved beach surrounded by black rocks glistening from the hot pool's rising steam. "It's so beautiful, John, and so much more vivid and real than my dream portrayed."

He pointed upward at the craggy ceiling. "That's the shaft that vents out over the cliffs." A trickle of light beamed through a tiny cavity and washed over the pool's glassy, darkened surface. "As a lad, I wriggled through only far enough to see what beckoned below."

"I can't believe you fell from the cliffs as I did. So much for not keeping any secrets, huh?" She brushed gritty sand from her teal skirts and a stringy cobweb from her arm.

"Nor can I believe you escaped the guardsmen's watchful eye and ended up in the sea." He removed his sword belt, propped it against a rock and divested himself of his wrist daggers. His dark brown hair wisped with golden ends lay slick on his shoulders as he crouched at the water's edge and swirled a hand through. Waves rippled across the stillness.

"I didn't mean to worry you. I'm sorry. It's just that I can be a little sneaky, and now you've had fair warning." She unlaced her gown's front stays, dragged her arms out of the long, clingy sleeves then shimmied her teal skirts over her hips and onto the ground. She picked up the wet mess, wrung it out and laid it overtop one of the boulders at the rear of the cave to dry.

"Is everything still the same as you saw it in your dream?" John stared at her, so hungrily.

"So close as to almost be the same." She rolled her sark's clammy sleeves to the elbow, dipped her toes into the water then waded in. Her ankle-length white linen shift tangled around her legs as she lowered to her chest in the deliciously warm water. "I did though refrain last night from telling you about certain things."

"As in…"

"This sark hinders me when I swim. In my time, women wear swimsuits and such."

"And what is a swimsuit?" He perched on a rock and tugged off his boots.

"It's a small suit of clothing one wears in the water that allows fluid movement." She lifted her sark's hem over her head and tossed it onto the sand where it hit with a resounding slap.

John's hands stilled on the fastening of his white tunic's ties. He lifted his gaze and ogled the mop of wet linen. "You unclothed yourself?"

"I'm wearing the equivalent of a two-piece swimsuit underneath. My bra and panties will do as a bikini. A girl can't give up all her favorite pieces of clothing when she travels to the past. Anyway, it's dark and I'm underneath the water. Just strip off and hop in." She winked at him. "You do, with very little persuasion by the way."

"You tempt me beyond my endurance." He shucked his tunic, leaving his black leather pants on as he strode toward her. His wide chest held a smattering of hair, the same dark shade as his head. Thick biceps bulged as he dove in. Underneath the water, he swam then emerged a mere breath before her. "Aye, 'tis dark enough. I see naught."

"Trust me. You've nothing to fear from my underwear. Let me show you." She caught his hands, slid them around her waist. "As I told you in my dream, a bra has two pieces of fabric which cover a woman's breasts and—"

"Oh hell." He stretched his hands, spanned her bare skin more fully. "Your belly is exposed."

"And my legs." She eased his hands down her sides, over the thin silk edges of her pink panties and along her thighs. "But everything important is covered."

"'Tis becoming far too difficult to keep my hands off you."

"I like it when you touch me, and far too much." She rested her cheek on his chest and allowed the heavy beat of his heart to soothe her. "All I know is I can't allow what's happened between us, this soul bond, to change your future. An affair is still on the table, although a very short one."

"Katherine, when I sailed toward Dunyvaig, I sensed something was wrong. My chest throbbed and my soul ached. 'Twas as if I knew you needed me, just as I did this morn. Mayhap I need to show you exactly what I wish for, because that wish is for you." The clear surface rippled as he backed her toward the pool's rocky edge. Hands on her waist, he lifted her onto the ledge, heaved himself up beside her and tipped her onto her back. His gaze swept her body, his eyes gleaming molten gold in the near dark. "I want the right to touch you, as freely as any man does with his woman."

"I'm not your woman."

"Aye, you are, and I intend to prove it." He swept his hands over her midriff, fingers brushing the undersides of her breasts. "Your skin is so soft, and this fabric you wear so sheer. It clings to you."

"One night. How about we just enjoy this one night?" She couldn't hold herself away from him any longer. Back arched, she released the hooks and peeled her bra away. Her nipples beaded, wet and shiny as steam swirled around her.

"Ah, my sweet imp, when it comes to you, I lose all reason." He cupped her breasts and weighed them in his hands before easing them together. Slowly, he licked her nipple and the hot stroke of his tongue sent a bolt of heat straight to her core.

"You do the same to me."

He swirled around the tip. "You taste divine."

"If you missed it, I'm saying yes. Show me what it's like to join as one." He sucked her nipple deep into his mouth and a torrent of tingles raced through her. She grabbed his shoulders and clung. "Oh, that feels sooo good."

"I ache for what you offer." He thumbed her nipples, playing with them as he stared into her eyes. "But I need more than a moment of pleasure or a short affair."

"Please, don't ask any more than what I can give you." She trailed a finger along the waistband of his leather pants and loosened the ties. "Let's enjoy this time and not think about the future. Make love to me."

"You make it impossible to say nay, but I do intend to prove you're mine." He gripped his waistband and shoved his leather pants down his thickly muscled legs and off. His cock bobbed free and brushed his belly, one very large cock with a plump head darkening to a delectable rosy color.

"Well, now at least I know exactly what you've been hiding under your kilt."

"That you do, lass." Chuckling, he knelt between her legs and his balls drew tighter and higher into the thatch of dark brown curls covering the apex of his groin. Gently, he tucked his leather pants under her, providing a soft cushioning against the rock. "Allow me to give you pleasure first."

"I want to touch you too."

"Aye, wherever you please."

She traced the ridged bands of his stomach. Hard muscles honed to perfection made her mouth water. And his abs, they rippled as she brushed the head of his cock. Carefully, she fondled the tip and stroked to the root. "You feel so hard, yet your skin is smooth like velvet."

"I wish for you to know all of my body, as I wish to know all of yours." He skimmed his warm hands along her outer thighs and heat raced across the path he touched. He lifted her bottom and caressed her cheeks then slowly, he slid his fingers under the fabric of her panties and tugged them down. He puffed hotly against her belly as he whispered, "You're my woman, my faerie."

"I am, for tonight." She'd take what he offered and cherish the memory forever.

"Nay, no' only for tonight. For always." Eyes twinkling, he embraced her breasts, kissing and licking until she arched into him. He took her nipple between his lips and rolled his tongue around it.

With her hips pushing against his, she clutched his broad shoulders, swept her hands over his roped biceps and down his arms. So big and strong. Needing to touch all of him, she stroked his smooth back and tapered waist. Her warrior protector was built to battle and conquer, and right now, he was doing a fine job with her. He sucked her nipples, both soothing the need deep within her and inflaming an equal need for more. Surrounding her, hot and hard, he intensified that heat.

"I have other places to devour." He dipped his fingers

between them and glided along the inside of her thigh. "Say, aye. I need your agreement afore I go further."

"You can have all the agreement you wish for." Craving a deeper touch, she eased her legs apart. Her mind raced in a hundred different directions but they all led to one place. "Don't stop."

"I'll never hurt you. Do you trust me?" He swept his hand over her entrance, his intimate touch scalding her.

"With my very soul."

"Then we will be one." He plunged one finger inside, stroked deep then curled his finger into a spot that had her almost catapulting off the ledge and she would have if he hadn't been holding her down. "This is just the beginning." Head bent, he kissed along her inner thigh, his breath hot on her skin as he rubbed her clit.

"Please, yes please." Eyes closed, she sank her fingers into his hair and massaged his scalp. Oh, John was about to take her places she'd never dreamed of. "More."

"Look at me, Katherine. I want to see to your pleasure."

"I want to see yours too." She looked into his eyes, then reached down and skimmed the hard length of his cock. Caressing his hot flesh, she pumped him in time with how he stroked her.

He moaned, long and low, the sensual sound thrilling her as he slid lower. Then he spread her legs even wider and licked her flesh in the most intimate way. Every flick of his tongue over her clit was such exquisite torture.

She'd died once, and it appeared she was about to die again.

* * * *

John wanted Katherine with a thirst he'd never known, and saying no to her had been impossible. He'd longed for her since the moment she'd fallen through the veil and into his arms. Since that time, their bond had only strengthened further. He wouldn't lose her. Not ever.

After raising her legs, he hooked them over his shoulders until her bottom lifted off the ledge and she lay even more fully exposed to him. "You're beautiful, so pink and lush." He parted her folds and plunged his tongue deep inside her. She bucked, her nipples hardening into tight points. "I see you like that."

"I have a feeling I'll like everything you do." She gasped for breath.

"Then I shall make that my mission." Lapping her, he eased two fingers in as he gently stretched her. Sensations stormed him and his cock throbbed as he imbibed at the very heart of her.

"John, that feels too good. Kiss me. I need your mouth on mine."

He lifted up, took her mouth in a hot kiss as he continued to stroke his fingers into her below. As he did, she caressed his cock with long pulls and his spine tingled as the pressure in his shaft built to a crescendo. "I cannae hold on if you do that."

"Then come inside me."

"Aye, that I long for." He kissed her again, covering her mouth with his and demanding a response that would distract her mind, then with his hands on her hips, he lifted her to him and moved between her legs. He teased his cock along her slick folds. "Open wider for me."

She spread her legs farther. "I know there'll be a little pain. I can handle it. I want this so don't stop."

"Naught can halt me now." His cock brushed against her thin barrier and his mind went dark with lust. She was his, for all time. Now, his mission would be to convince her of that. Claiming her, he tore through her innocence and plunged deep inside her hot channel.

"Oh." She gasped against his lips, clutched his butt and urged him to go faster. "That feels so good, as if there isn't a part of me not filled with you."

"You're mine." Frantically, he kissed her, pounding harder and deeper as their connection consumed him. Her soft moans encouraged him, and he took her wildly.

"I feel too much." She raked his back then cried his name.

He was lost as her inner muscles tightened and dragged him in. His thoughts flew and his release exploded violently along with hers. Deep within, he spilled his seed.

"My woman," he whispered and kissed her luscious lips. "I'll never join with another. You're a part of me, as I'm a part of you. We belong together, and I intend to prove it."

* * * *

The wave of pleasure sweeping through Katherine had her struggling to gain a decent breath. This was heaven, and she never wanted their time together to end, not now, not ever. Flashes of white still burst behind her closed eyelids as her channel pulsed around John's cock, over and over. It was too much, yet not enough. "I want more."

John's lips lifted, every inch of his body fully aligned with hers. "You'll be sore if I give you more."

"Right now, I don't care." She caressed the corded muscles of his damp back. "I love the feel of you on top of me, inside me. I never want to forget this moment."

"Are you certain?" His breath tickled her ear. "I dinnae wish to hurt you."

"Very certain. In fact, I dare you to show me what else you can do."

"Well, I adore a dare." He rocked his hips and his shaft stirred and lengthened inside her.

"Mmm, I can feel every little movement you make." She cradled his face in her hands, brought his mouth back to hers and kissed him. "I love it."

"Then I shall make it my mission to pleasure you. I want you to reach for the stars again and fly." He chuckled then rocked faster.

"Great plan. I'm totally on board." She sighed as he continued to rise and fill her. "We're one and nothing has ever felt so right."

"I'll never relinquish you."

His words sent a thrill through her, and his next kiss took her places she more than desired. Below, he stroked deep, his shaft hot and slick as he pumped within her. She wanted more, and as much as he could give her in whatever time they had left. As he increased his rhythm, he rubbed her clit. Oh, sooo good. She moved with him as he pushed his long length in then out, his kisses matching the same ebb and flow as below.

Her orgasm built. "Too fast. I want this moment to last forever."

"Nay, I need to hear you scream my name." He grinned and with her breasts bobbing so close to his lips, he suctioned his mouth around one tight bud and sucked, hard.

She came, crying out his name and convulsing around him. She rode the waves as his seed jetted inside her, her heartbeat a pounding mess against his. A more perfect union she'd never known.

Peace invaded her, to the depths of her soul.

* * * *

John rolled onto his side, taking the brunt of his weight off Katherine.

"Where are you going?" She wrapped her arms around his neck and clung to him.

"I'm too heavy and this ledge is hard." He tipped her over and smoothed his hand down her back. Her creamy skin appeared a little pink but bore no scrapes. He settled her back on top of his leather trews which had protected her from the stone. "Next time, I shall ensure there is a bed."

"Will you now?" Her seductive tone, so achingly sweet, caused his cock to twitch with life again. Hell, he should be well sated by now. He'd certainly never returned to life so quickly before. 'Twas a shame the cavern had darkened further and little light now shone through the vent. Night was falling and they needed to return.

"They'll be a bed and I shall see to it. For now we must leave."

"This place is so special." In a saucy swirl, she trailed a finger down the center of his chest. "Honestly, I'd rather stay here."

"As would I, but 'tis best we return." He picked up the scrap of material she'd called panties, and on his knees, slid them up her legs to her knees. Her soft flesh and bare mound made his cock pulse with need. When he'd first removed her underwear and seen the smoothness, he'd almost come right then and there. He touched the smear of blood along her inner thighs and his chest pumped out. She'd given him her innocence, the right allowed only to her husband. Whether she realized it or not, the precious gift was one he'd now claimed and would honor to his dying day.

"What are you thinking?" Her blue eyes softened. "You've a very possessive look in your eyes."

"I crave you." He needed to take care with his words and not push her too hard. She had no of intention of changing his future path even though he certainly intended it. He'd give her time, sway her gently to his way of thinking.

Leaning over the ledge, he scooped hot water from the pool. Tenderly, he washed her clean, and once done, tugged her panties up and pressed a soft kiss against the pink satin.

"I crave you too." She stroked along his hip, dipped down and palmed his balls. His cock surged to life, and when she eyed the tip and dipped her head, he shuddered with need.

Oh hell, he would never be able to stop her if—

She licked him with one long teasing stroke of her tongue then settled her lips over the head and took him deep.

"Katherine." He jerked as her sweet mouth seared him.

"I need this." She caressed the top of his sac, her fingers sliding so sensuously around him. 'Twas torture, unlike any he'd ever suffered before.

"Halt," he croaked.

She sucked harder and he rocked his hips, pushing deeper inside her mouth. He should stop her. He should pull out. A sexual haze consumed him and he shoved the crotch of her panties to one side and impaled himself within her delicious heat.

"Yes," she cried out, her shoulders lifting off the rock at the fast impact of their joining.

He stretched her, fighting for control as he thrust in and out.

"I want this. Harder." Her voice, raw and needy, had him moving faster.

"There was supposed to be a bed," he growled as he rolled them over until she came up on top. "Ride me, and dinnae stop."

"No stopping." She gasped as she moved up and down. "Ohh, nooo stopping."

"I'm going to lose my mind."

"I want you to lose more than that." She tipped her head back, her silky blond hair trailing behind her and onto his legs as she picked up her speed.

The intensity of the moment shook him. Grasping her hips, he rocked them harder until her tight channel hugged him all the way to his balls.

"John, I'm—"

"Let go. I'm right here with you."

"Oh, oh yes," she cried out as she pulsed around him.

With no choice, he came hard, shattering right along with her.

"Ahh, wonderful," she murmured then drooped on top of him, her breasts mashed between them.

"More like magnificent." He couldn't move. 'Twas as if she'd drained his life's blood, and not on the battlefield, but within the magical cavern he'd found as a lad. This place had always entranced him, and now he adored it even more so. He'd never forget this moment, or the depth of satisfaction that consumed him, heart, body, and soul. "You wield the ultimate power over me."

"I do?" She dragged her gaze to his and smiled. "Care to elaborate?"

"'Tis best I dinnae."

She wriggled her hips, and he groaned. "Oh, I believe I've found the power."

"Cheeky, lass." He swatted her bottom. "Remain still."

"All right, but only because you asked so nicely." She spread her palm over his heart then lowered her cheek to his chest and sighed. "I truly love the sound of your heartbeat."

He wrapped his arms around her and closed his eyes as the steamy air created a sultry haven.

Warm and soothing, her breath whispered across his skin as she went lax and fell asleep. A little rest wouldn't hurt either of them. A few minutes, no more.

He allowed sleep to claim him.

Chapter 5

A pretty bird's trill drifted into the cavern from outside and John stirred. He blinked his eyes open and squinted at the sliver of sunlight beaming through the vent above. 'Twas morning, and Katherine lay tucked against his side, wearing only her pink panties and her skin warm from the steamy heat swirling through the cavern.

"Sleepy," she mumbled as she nuzzled his neck. "Need more sleep."

"'Tis morn. They'll be a party out searching for us if we dinnae return soon." He eased away from her, hooked his legs over the side of the ledge and slid into the water. If he remained next to Katherine while she remained so underdressed, they'd never leave this place. He dunked his head and came up, water sluicing down his face. "In you get. We need to wash, dress, and be away."

She stood on the ledge and stretched her arms high, her breasts swaying, full and heavy. Her nipples, a sweet rose color, were the same luscious shade as her pouty lips. She nabbed her bra, donned it then flapped out his trews. "These are half dry. Gosh, I slept right through the night without waking. No nightmares and no visions." A smile lit her face. "Making love to you obviously agrees with me."

"I know it agrees with me."

She laughed then glanced at the ledge where it met the black boulders. After bunching his trews into a ball, she inched onto the first boulder and tossed them. They flew in a wide arc through the air and landed with a soft plop on the sand. "You can thank me for the dry clothing later."

"Wet clothing does no' bother me." Daily training involved long ocean swims, conditioning him against the elements. He was more often wet than not. "Come bathe with me."

"This'll be fun. I've never bathed with a man before." She scrambled off the rock and into the water. It wasn't deep where she stood closer to the beach, the water only rising to her waist, but she slid under the surface and then emerged, her blond hair streaming over her shoulders and hiding her perfect breasts.

He slogged toward her, flicked her hair away and stroked one nipple through the almost transparent satin bra until the tip puckered into a tight ball. "I fear I'll never get my fill of you."

"Take what you wish, John. While we're here in this cavern, I'm all yours." She clasped his face. "Please, kiss me. I don't want you to hold back, not here."

Hell, she held such a potent enchantment he couldn't resist. Holding her close, he brushed his lips across hers and memories surged from the night before, of their shared passion and joining. One kiss would never be enough, but 'twas all he had time to take for now. Aye, he'd break down her defenses, wooing her as she deserved until she gave in to what he already knew to be the truth. They would be together, forever, and not only for one single night. He just had to convince her of that.

"You make me feel too hot." She rubbed her chest against his, her nipples, so incredibly hard, scraping across his flesh. "I want to stay."

"I wish we could, but 'tis best we dinnae cause an uproar and we've been gone from Dunyvaig long enough." He released her and waded into shore. After swiping his trews, he shook the sand out, jammed them on and collected his tunic and boots.

Katherine joined him. She tipped her head to the side, wrung the water from her hair then tugged her teal gown over her head. The crinkled velvet skimmed her hips and fell in a whoosh to her ankles. "So, what's the plan for today?"

"For you to remain safe at Dunyvaig while I continue searching for the MacLean warrior. If he's on Islay, I'll find him." He strapped on his sword belt and wrist daggers.

"I can't live my life trapped behind Dunyvaig's stone walls. That's not a life at all." She laced her gown's front stays to the top of the square-cut neckline trimmed with a white ribbon, slid her matching slippers on and wandered across to the tunnel. Using the rock wedged half under it, she clambered up and into the darkened shaft.

He grabbed her damp sark from the sand and followed her along the tunnel carved of stone until the crashing sounds of the waterfall and life beyond their secret haven echoed toward him. The passageway thinned and ahead, Katherine wedged herself sideways to fit through the thin slit in the rocks. After wriggling through, he joined her on the slick rock ledge where a clear sheet of water arched over them and pounded into the pool below.

"This place is so magical." She pressed herself against the wall as spray misted lightly. Morning sunshine glimmered through the water and sent a kaleidoscope of beautiful yellows, pinks and blues dancing over her sweet face.

"We'll return as often as my duties permit. I give you my word on that." He stroked a finger under her chin and dropped a kiss on the tip of her nose.

"You shouldn't be making promises like that to me, not that I don't appreciate your offer."

"You're still insistent you willnae change my future?"

"Absolutely."

Except she already had, not that he was prepared to tell her and do battle over it right now. She'd learn soon enough of his intentions to woo her in the coming days. With his hand on her lower back, he guided her to the end of the ledge. Below, white water tumbled over wide gray boulders, the river flowing fuller and swifter from the recent rains.

"It's like an art form in motion, nature at its most chaotic and singing of life."

"Aye, and we shall respect its life." He took a step back and leaped onto the grassy bank.

"Wait for me." She followed his lead and grinning, jumped.

He caught her with a chuckle and swung her down beside him. "You need to give me more warning afore you do that."

"Nope, I prefer to keep you on your toes." She twirled, her damp blond locks streaming behind her and her flushed cheeks and skin glowing. Her blue eyes captivated him, the color like precious sapphires with their deep glittering hue. An ethereal glow encircled her, as one had after her mother's visit. Aye, she was part fae, and she'd certainly cast a heavenly spell over him.

"I fear your mischievous ways will be difficult to tame."

"That's right. No taming for you." She patted his chest, right over his heart. "Why the wistfulness?"

"I've been entrusted with a piece of your soul and I never intend to relinquish it. Come, or I shall drag you back inside." He led the way through the forest alive with the twittering of birds and the rustling of small creatures hurrying through the undergrowth. As they neared the hunting trail, horses' hooves pounded toward them.

Archie galloped around the corner, his padded leather war coat donned and claymore strapped to his back. Half a dozen men rode behind him, all prepared for battle. Damn. His brother's scowl couldn't hide his worry. He should've returned last night.

Pulling his horse to a stop in a cloud of whirling autumn leaves, Archie eyed him. "Were you forced to find shelter from the storm?"

"Aye. We found somewhere safe to spend the night."

Archie's destrier snorted foggy air and he patted his mount's neck and calmed the beast. "The party of men you sent out into the forest yesterday returned afore the storm with word they'd found tracks. We ride, no' only to find you, but to continue the search for our enemy." He extended his hand to Katherine. "We didnae bring a spare horse. You'll need to ride with me. Marie awaits your return."

Katherine glanced at him and he nodded. "Go with Archie. I'll be right behind you." He boosted her into the saddle in front of his brother then doubled up with another warrior. After they returned to Dunyvaig, he intended to ride out with the party in search of Finlay MacLean. Aye, the sooner he removed the threat against Katherine, the sooner he could return to her.

They pounded down the trail, branches brushing his arms as the path thinned before they burst out of the forest and galloped across the moors toward the castle with its ever-watchful guardsmen patrolling the barbican.

Katherine peeked at him over Archie's arm and rubbed her reddened nose.

"Are you cold?" he called out.

"Only a little."

They rode under the arched entrance and into the inner courtyard. He jumped to the ground, strode to Archie and swung Katherine down beside him.

Archie dismounted and whistled to a stable lad. "Saddle John's destrier and ensure he has adequate supplies."

"My thanks. I willnae be long." He clapped Archie on the back then steered Katherine inside. He bypassed the great hall where his clan had gathered to break their fast and led her up the winding side stairs. At his chamber on the third-floor, he ushered her in and shut the door.

"I want to come with you." She squeezed her hands,

making tiny fists, her knuckles white with the strain.

"Nay, you'll remain here." He shucked his tunic, swiped his coal black shirt from his trunk and hauled it on. With clean trews and his padded leather cotun donned, he strapped his weapons on and gathered his bow and satchel of arrows from behind his chunky corner desk.

Katherine watched him as she edged from foot to foot. "You look like you're readying for war. I don't like it. It feels wrong."

"One must take every precaution when there are MacLeans about."

"I only saw one MacLean, and now I wish I'd never told you about him. I've no desire to escalate this war, and with you on the hunt for him, that's exactly what I've done."

"You must never think that. 'Tis my right and duty to protect you." He grabbed his traveling bag, flipped the top leather flap and stuffed a change of clothes inside.

"How long will you be gone?"

"As long as it takes." He crossed to her, slid a hand under her hair and around her nape. "The guardsmen will be under orders to ensure you dinnae leave these walls. You've yet to give me your word you'll remain."

"You can't bully me into submission, John." Clearly frustrated, she jerked away.

"If you followed my orders when given, I wouldnae have to demand your submission." He detested having to leave her this way, but Archie waited. He strode to the door with his gear. With one last look over his shoulder, he gritted out, "Be here when I return, and that's an order."

"You're also not allowed to order me about." She crossed her arms. "You need to worry more about yourself. My life depends on your survival, so if you get hurt, so do I."

"Aye, I'll take all care." He desperately wished to wrap his arms around her and offer what comfort he could, but now was not the time. "Stay safe, my love."

"I'm not your love." She straightened her spine. "We've had nothing more than one night, and it'll probably have to remain that way."

"Trust me. We'll have plenty more. I must go." He marched out of his chamber, his gut gnawing in the most vicious way with each step he took away from her. Leaving her was pure agony.

"Captain." George joined him as he strode outside and into the bailey. "Any orders while you're gone?"

"Aye, watch Katherine for me, like a hawk." He strapped his bag onto his steed and checked the cinch. "She acts without thought for herself and you'll need to keep a vigilant eye on her."

"Will do, Captain."

"Inform the sentry to bar the postern gate and be alert to all who come and go through the main entrance. When she retires for the night, remain on guard outside her door." He slid into the saddle. "Be assured, if aught happens to her while I'm gone, your head will roll."

"I'll see to your orders. All will be as you've asked." George dipped his head and stepped back.

He trusted his man. George wouldn't fail him.

Archie brought his stallion in beside him. "What worries you, John?"

"My woman intends to travel to Mull. She visited the circle and one of the fae spoke to her, instructing her to complete what Marie has set in motion. She's certain she must bring peace between the clans."

He snorted. "'Tis an impossible task, and Marie has already told me there will be no peace between the clans for some years to come. Katherine must have misheard."

"She does no' believe so." Although he'd discuss it with her further, the moment he returned. For now, he had an enemy warrior to find. He nudged his horse and with Archie at his side, galloped out the gates, their men riding in file behind them. He'd never allow Katherine to journey beyond Islay's shores. Losing her to her MacLean kin would never happen, not on his watch.

* * * *

Two days John had been gone and without any word on how his hunt for Finlay MacLean fared, Katherine's nerves were frayed. She gripped the stone windowsill of the ladies' solar window as Marie and Mary sat behind her in padded forest-green chairs either side of the roaring fire.

"Are you all right, Katherine?" Marie pinned cream satin cups into place on the bra she'd made.

"I will be, when John gets back." She needed a distraction from her frustrating thoughts.

"I worry too when the men are away." Mary sighed. "'Tis difficult to always be the one waiting." She continued repairing a rip in the sleeve of an embroidered tunic.

"It's at times like these, I miss cell phones." Marie glanced at Katherine. "Do you still have yours on you? You took a snap of us that day I traveled. Did you keep it in your pocket?"

"I did. I fell through the veil with it, but John took it away from me the other day when I showed him. He buried it somewhere in the forest. Said he didn't wish for anyone to find it and question me." Arms crossed, she huffed and pressed her bottom against the windowsill. "Can you believe he did that? I was still paying my iphone off on a twenty-four month plan. An iphone. No one in their right mind buries an iphone."

"What's an iphone, Katherine?" Mary's eyes lit with interest as she asked her. Whenever they mentioned something from the future, she always asked about it, and she adored Mary's excitement.

"It's a device that fits in the palm of your hand. You hold it, either to your ear, or press the speaker button, and it picks up your voice. You can use it to talk to anyone in the world, provided they've got the same kind of device at their end."

"Anyone in the world?" Her mouth dropped open. "Surely you jest?"

"Nope. They're a relatively new device. Cell phones have only been around for twenty-five years or so."

"How incredible." Mary tilted her head toward Marie as she sewed. "And that bra you're making looks so intriguing. When did that item of underwear first become available?"

"I'm not sure, but the French first called this a brassiere. The corsets the ladies of this time wear, lift the breasts quite well and taper the waist in, but the bra molds only the breasts and allows a greater freedom of movement around the midsection. I can't be without one."

"The fabric is so soft." She reached across and fingered the satin. "And so pretty."

"If you'd like, I'll make you one next. Perhaps a nursing bra first." Marie picked up a swathe of padded white linen from Mary's fabric basket. "I'll include this padding in front of the satin so it captures any leakage."

"Oh, wonderful." Mary beamed.

Katherine let out a long breath, pushed off the windowsill and paced the solar, from tapestry covered wall to wall. "I hate the way John and I parted."

"You can't change what's happened." Marie's gaze softened. "He's worried about you, and I'm not surprised considering the fae's request. Even I know it's only a matter of time before you find a way to escape George."

"You sound like you agree with the fact John's all but made me housebound."

"No, but"—she scratched her head—"I still don't understand why the fae asked you to bring about peace, not when peace doesn't come for some years."

"You think I should ignore their request?"

"Honestly, no. It's best that you don't, although you'll need to take great care when you travel to Mull. I feel as if there's more to this mission than what you've been told."

"Same, but I can't do a thing about it while I'm stuck here on Islay. Somehow I have to escape my guard, then figure out the rest when I get to Duart." She scrubbed her face. "I miss him, badly. I never thought my feelings for him would grow so strong, or so quickly."

"Then use this time to give yourself some breathing space."

"He's done that with his leaving." Didn't her sister understand? "He holds a piece of my soul, Marie. Our bond goes far deeper than I ever thought possible. Being with him is so soothing, like I've come home." She stopped at the window and rubbed her achy chest. The forest beckoned, because somewhere out there, John roamed. "It hurts to know he's meant for another." The pain worsened as it sliced through her.

"Do you mean Madison MacDonald?" Mary cleared her throat.

"Pardon?" She spun about. "Who's Madison MacDonald?"

"Oh, I'm so sorry. I presumed you knew. You said it hurts to know he's meant for another."

"Yes, but I didn't actually know there was already another? Who on earth is Madison?"

"Allow me to tell you about her. Three years past, Angus spoke to John and Archie about his desire to have one of his captains wed his second cousin from Skye and strengthen the bonds between the two MacDonald clans. Madison is Evan MacDonald's eldest daughter and she lives at Dunscaith, although the lass was only thirteen at the time. Archie gave Angus an adamant no and said he would never take a wife, so John stepped forward and agreed to the match."

"Why didn't he say anything?" He'd never mentioned a word to her.

"Mayhap he's forgotten." Mary set her mending down. "With the feud and Angus's capture, all talks were laid aside."

"Are such talks binding?"

"Naught has been formally contracted, but aye, John's verbal agreement to a marriage could be considered binding in itself."

Goodness, and now three years had passed. The girl would be sixteen, old enough to wed in this day and age.

"Katherine?" Deep compassion swam in Marie's gaze. "Are you all right?"

Numb, she nodded. "At least I now know who he's meant for." She knelt at Mary's feet, her burgundy skirts billowing around her. "Tell me more about Madison."

"I've no' seen her in three years, but at the time I thought her a spritely lass with her wide smile and auburn hair. Being the eldest, she aids her mother with her younger siblings. She'll make him a fine wife."

Mary's words roared in her ears. "I—I want him to have a fine wife," she whispered.

"Katherine, you're crying." Marie wrapped an arm around her shoulders. "Everything will be all right."

"John is promised to another." She wiped her wet cheeks. "He'll never be mine." Although maybe this was exactly what she'd needed to hear. The fae had given her a mission and she had to leave, and preferably before John returned.

"I know what you're thinking." Marie hugged her. "You want to leave, except you're supposed to keep him close. The fae told you so."

"Yes, but he's made it abundantly clear he hates all things MacLean. I've no choice but to leave, and I'll need your help. I can't sneak out of here without aid."

"You'll always have my aid." She breathed a long sigh. "I can't believe I'm going to help send you away."

"Allow me to aid you as well. I believe in your mission, Katherine." Mary rummaged through the basket of clothing still needing repair. "You're a MacLean and you wear my amulet. Once you reach Mull, tell the MacLeans I sent you. Many of the warriors we fought against at the Rhinns saw Marie and you're her identical. Allow them to assume you are her. No one would harm one of the fae."

"I can do that."

"Good. Also, seek my brother's wife out. Margaret cared for James and she has a kind heart."

"I promise I'll seek her out, only how do I get to Mull?"

"Make your way along the coastline to Ardbeg. The seaside village is close and once you reach it, you can hire one of the fishermen to sail you across the waterway. They willnae wish to make landfall for long, but I have my own coin and I'll give you what you need to ensure your safe passage." She hauled a lad's fawn-colored tunic, breeches, and cap from the basket and passed it to her. "I made these for James, but he's yet to grow into them. This clothing should fit you and provide an adequate disguise. We need to sneak you out of here."

"Now, that's a plan I can work with." Excitement and trepidation rolled through her in equal measure. Leaving for Mull was right, the reason she was here. Quickly, she unlaced her gown, donned the lad's clothing and bundled her hair up under the cap. Mary passed her a pair of socks and boots. She tugged them on and twirled around. "How do I look?"

"You'll need a plaid to keep you warm, one that does no' hold the MacDonald colors." Mary searched inside her basket and grinned as she pulled out a black and white tartan. She wrapped it around her waist and secured it with a pin across her chest. "Now, you look perfect."

"I'll fetch supplies from the kitchen and pack you a bag." Marie dashed to the door in a flurry of emerald skirts. "I won't be long." She snuck out.

"I'll see to the fae's mission. I won't fail them, or you, Mary."

"I know you willnae, but please, take care." Mary crossed to her corner desk and opened a drawer. She returned and pressed several coins into her hand. "This should see you through."

"Thank you. I'd like to write John a note." She pocketed the coins then picked up a quill and a piece of paper from Mary's desk. She explained to him her reason for going and that she hadn't wished to leave under such circumstances, but she'd return, as soon as her mission was complete and that he wasn't to worry about her. After signing her name, she blew on the wet ink and once it dried, folded the letter in three. "Could you give this to him for me?"

"Of course." Mary slid it into her olive gown's pocket.

"I've got everything you need." Marie rushed back into the room, her cheeks flushed and a wooden pail in hand. "George just popped out to the bailey. He's overseeing the change of guard so now's the perfect time for you to leave."

"I take it I'm to collect the fish for the day?"

"That you are." She passed her the pail holding a brown canvas satchel hidden inside. "The cook's son was about to head down to the bay to collect the fishermen's catch. I told him I would ask another to see to the task. With Mary's help, we'll get you out of here, or at least that's the plan."

* * * *

Ten minutes later Katherine swung her pail in one hand as she ambled across the bailey, her gait the same as the cook's son's lanky stride. Across the keep near the center well, Mary and Marie walked then stopped. Mary gasped then with an anguished moan, bent over. Mary's cry tore at her, made her want to drop her pail and run to her, but she held her place.

The guards raced toward Mary and Marie, George at the front.

The moment they passed Katherine, she dashed out the gate and raced into the forest. Her sister could be as sneaky as her, and it appeared her ancestor as well.

Once clear of the guardsmen's sight, she followed the trail

until the crashing of the ocean's waves reached her on the breeze. Veering toward the sea, she scrambled down a stony track and onto the beach. Behind her, Dunyvaig stood like a sentinel perched on the tip of Lagavulin Bay.

Time to complete her mission. She straightened her shoulders and firmed her resolve. Ardbeg was only a few miles away. She'd get there, find a fisherman and sail to Mull.

As she trekked, seagulls circled overhead. One squawked then dove into the white-capped waves and emerged with a fish. Its catch drew the attention of the other birds and they flew after it. Past the screeching cacophony and across the waterway, Mull and her MacLean kin awaited her. Hopefully her father's clan would embrace her and not turn her away.

Goodness. Was she truly leaving the safety of Dunyvaig for the unknown of Duart? Her step slowed as worry skittered through her. No, this was right. She had to continue on.

The sun dipped along the horizon and sent a final flare of red across the sunset sky. The wind blasted through and she shivered. Ahead, the bay curved and a stream gurgled into the sea. She clambered over the rocks, lowered herself to her knees at the brook's edge and dipped her hands into the stream and sipped. Icy water hit her empty belly and she swayed.

"Well, well, who do we have here?" A scraggly bearded warrior stepped out of the gloominess of the tree line, his grass-stained tattered tunic smeared with blood. His gaze moved over her then to the amulet glinting at her neck. "The faerie, the one we captured and took to the Rhinns. This is a boon finding you."

"You're Finlay?" He looked exactly as he had in her vision.

"Aye." His bushy brown brows drew together. "It appears you're a clever faerie too. 'Tis no wonder my chief wanted you."

"I might be fae, but I'm also of both clans, MacLean and MacDonald."

"That worries me no'. Lachlan chose you as the bait to lure the MacDonalds into a battle, and so will I, except on MacLean land where we'll have a greater fighting force."

"I'll never aid you in your war, not when the fae have given me the task to bring about some peace."

"There will never be peace." He spat on the ground. "You have the power to aid us in the return of our land, and even though Lachlan was taken by the king's men following our battle, I willnae give up his fight. As my hostage, you'll provide me with bargaining power I need over the MacDonalds. The Rhinns will be ours. Make no mistake about that." He grabbed her arm and hauled her after him. Hidden within bushes at the bend in the bay, a half-beached skiff sat waiting. He tossed her into the hull, pushed the boat into the water and sprayed drops over her as he bounded in.

Even though John had searched this area and now scoured the woods for Finlay, he hadn't changed history. Finlay had found her, and with the Isle of Mull now her destination, she didn't put up a fight. She would arrive at Duart by Finlay's hand, the future unchanged.

* * * *

As the sun dipped along the horizon, John crouched in the forest at the base of a tree next to Archie and their men. For the past two days, they'd searched the woods within five miles of Dunyvaig.

"These are the freshest tracks we've come across." Archie inspected the prints in the damp soil then stared upward. "It appears our adversary may have used the treetops to remain hidden."

Above, a rope made of vines looped around the tree's bow, gave evidence of that very fact. John nodded. "He slept in the bow, securing himself with the vines so as no' to fall."

"I'll take a closer look." Archie eyed Eric. "Give me a boost."

Eric, one of their best trackers, bent and cupped his hands. He was a massive man, yet one who had the uncanny ability of slipping in and out of the smallest spaces.

Archie planted his foot in Eric's palms and jumped as Eric heaved him upward. Archie knelt in the bow then peered across at the tree closest to him. He leaped and sailed through the air, from one tree to the next then when he could go no farther, he shimmied down the trunk and landed on the mossy ground with a soft clomp. Bending, he surveyed the area. "Here's where the tracks begin again."

"Damn it." John traipsed toward his brother. "Finlay MacLean is a snake. He knew exactly how to conceal himself."

"We'll find him, John. He cannae evade us forever."

"You're damn right we'll find—" Pain slammed through his chest and he stumbled to his knees.

"John?" Archie grasped his shoulder. "What's wrong?"

'Twas as if someone had taken a spear and thrust it right through his heart. He patted his back to be sure no one had attacked him from behind. The pain slowly receded but not the sheer ache in his soul. That could be only one thing. "'Tis Katherine. Something's happened to her. I have to go."

With one hand on the ground, he shoved to his feet then raced toward his tethered horse. Behind him, Archie ordered Eric and the others to continue following the warrior's tracks then sprinted after him.

John mounted and rode hard toward Dunyvaig. He urged his black destrier faster down the narrow forest path edging the cliffs. Below, the sea roared and crashed against the jagged rock wall.

White-hot terror cut through him. 'Twas as if his soul-deep connection with Katherine was stretching to its farthest point, tearing at his chest. Everything within him demanded he find her.

Fisting his horse's reins, he burst out of the forest and plunged down the hillside toward an isolated bay, the very one he'd searched following Katherine's nightmare, and the very one he checked again each day. Across the rocky beach a scrap of black and white tartan fluttered where it had snagged between two boulders, while out at sea a skiff's white sail caught the moonlight then disappeared in the dark toward the north.

"What it is?" Archie called as he rode in beside him.

"Katherine's gone. I can feel the depth of my loss through our bond. We need to sail to Mull." She was on that skiff, and he was certain of it. "The warrior has her."

He slammed his knees into his steed, jumped a fallen tree across his path and raced toward Dunyvaig. He'd make chase, and as quickly as he could.

Chapter 6

After two days of bitter wind in her face and a night on the cold ground when they'd stopped at the Isle of Jura's northern tip to rest, the sea journey to Mull was almost done.

Katherine huddled within her black and white plaid as Duart Castle rose like a fortress in the moonlight ahead. The MacLean stronghold sat prominently at the point where the Sound of Mull intersected with Loch Linne and the Firth of Lorne. Land rose from the water in every direction. The stronghold held a very favorable position with its unhindered views.

A few hundred feet inland, the castle's massive gray tower windows were lit with candlelight, its fortified walls topped with battlements and guardsmen roaming the ramparts. Lachlan MacLean's vast holdings stretched across several isles, from Mull to Jura and to Coll, yet this was his favored stronghold.

"We're almost there." Finlay lowered the sail and plunged his oars into the depths of the water as he maneuvered the skiff toward the sea-gate.

Near the stone landing, two large men waded into the water. Each seized a side of the skiff as they came abreast of them. They guided the boat the last few feet and nestled it next to the stone stairs.

Another warrior appeared out of the dark along the castle trail, his massive claymore strapped across his back. Dressed in black leather trews and an emerald silk tunic, the colors matched his midnight-black hair and vivid green eyes to perfection. The warrior eyed Finlay. "We thought you'd been captured. Welcome home, cousin."

"The MacDonalds searched for me, but I managed to evade them." He bounded onto the landing and gripped the warrior in a firm forearm hold then motioned toward her. "I've brought you a gift, Captain, a bargaining chip to be used against the MacDonalds."

The dark-haired warrior scrutinized her. "A bargaining chip? All I see a lass dressed in lad's clothing."

"This is Lachlan's faerie. She was there when we battled for the Rhinns."

The warrior edged forward, one thumb sliding under his claymore's front belted strap. "I wasnae there, but I heard Lachlan's faerie has long white-blond hair, that she came forth from the guardians' circle and is of both clans, her father a MacLean and her mother a MacDonald. I'll have your name, lass."

She fought the chill in her bones and stood to gain some height. "Katherine MacLean, and I was already on my way here when I met Finlay. I've come willingly, or willingly enough. I also won't be considered as a bargaining chip. I'm here to learn more about my MacLean kin." She tugged the cap from her head and her locks fell in a soft swish to her waist. "Here is your proof of who I am."

He watched her, one brow slowly rising then resting a hand on Finlay's shoulder, he said, "I understand why you would bring her here, but using women and children as pawns in our war bothers me. She's also a MacLean, one of our own. I'll need to think on what we're to do."

"Lachlan wouldnae think twice about it, Arthur. Using her as leverage to gain an advantage against the MacDonalds is imperative. Our numbers have been severely depleted from our last battle and we cannae win this war through the usual means."

"She is still a MacLean." Arthur stepped toward her and extended his hand. "It appears you'll be here to stay for a while. Welcome to Duart."

"Thank you." She tucked her bag over her shoulder and took his hand.

He swung her onto the landing beside him and her legs shook from being confined to one position for so long. "Are you well?" He kept a steadying hand on her elbow as she wobbled.

"I'm not used to being at sea or traveling for such a long length of time across water."

"Then come. You'll no doubt enjoy a warm bath and a meal." He led her across the pebbly beach and toward the trail. They followed the path up the grassy rise then strode past flickering torches mounted against the stone walls of the bailey.

From the direction of the entrance, a boisterous buzz of voices echoed toward her and she took a deep, fortifying breath and entered the great hall. The vaulted room held high wooden beamed rafters, and the walls were covered with beautiful tapestries, of hunting and landscape scenes. The sight of trestle tables stacked with platters of cooked meat, boiled eggs, and bread, made her empty belly rumble. On wooden benches, a good hundred warriors or more sat, while serving maids carrying trays holding steaming bowls of stew, weaved around them. This clan thrived even though they'd suffered the imprisonment of their chief and the loss of a number of their men in the recent battle.

"There's Margaret." Arthur urged her toward the dais where a woman stood, her gaze on them as they crossed the room. Margaret looked so similar to Mary with her pale complexion, freckled cheeks, and red-gold locks tumbling down to her waist, except this woman wasn't carrying as Mary was. Tall and lithe, her corseted red velvet gown hugged her trim waist, the red and gold silk ribbons lacing the front an entwining of rich colors. "The chief's wife will tend you during your stay, of which I shall decide the manner, and how long it shall be. Margaret." Arthur laid his hand on the woman's shoulder and gestured toward her. "Meet Lachlan's faerie, Katherine MacLean. She was present at the battle of the Rhinns, and Finlay has returned with her from Islay."

Margaret's eyes widened. "Arthur, please, dinnae tell me Finlay stole her away from the MacDonalds."

"She insists she came willingly."

"It's all right, I did." She stepped up to Margaret and lifted Mary's talisman for her to see. "This amulet is Mary's, recently gifted to me. She was most grateful for your kindness to her son while he remained here during the negotiations to free his father. Mary told me to seek you out."

She cast her gaze over the piece. "Aye, 'tis the same amulet she placed around her son's neck when she sent him here. Did my sister-by-marriage have another request of me?"

"I'm to ask you for aid."

"Then let's speak in private. Excuse us, Arthur." Margaret led her toward the stairwell then slowed as a maid walked toward her. "Maddie, I need you to prepare a bath for our guest, and be as quick as you can about it. Mistress Katherine's to have the blue chamber next to mine."

"Aye, my lady." The girl dashed upstairs.

"Margaret," Arthur called, his arms crossed and his booted feet planted wide. "I'll post a guard at her door. Our guest is no' permitted free reign to wander about Duart. With the laird away, I'm responsible for this clan and she has come forth from the MacDonalds' lair."

"Of course." Margaret tightened her grip on Katherine. "This way." She hurried up the winding stairs, guided her down a dimly lit passageway and slowed as ahead, two lanky lads with their shirttails fluttering loose over their breeches, heaved a tub through a doorway.

They entered the chamber and the lads set the tub down and shuffled out. Across the room, Maddie knelt at the hearth, coaxing the sparks of a welcoming fire into life. She added a log and it crackled and caught alight.

Rising, she dusted her hands against her aproned sides. "Is there aught more you need, my lady?"

Margaret nodded. "Aye, a tray, and to fetch some gowns from my ambry. It appears our guest has arrived with very little clothing."

Maddie bobbed her head and quietly closed the door behind her.

"Thank you. I had to leave Dunyvaig rather suddenly and I have just what's on me." She set the satchel with the meager supplies Marie had given her on the end of the four-poster bed with its rich burgundy velvet canopy. "I'm truly glad to be here."

"You may be fae, but you're also MacLean. I dinnae wish for you to fear during your stay with us." Looking into her eyes, Margaret squeezed her hands, her fingers warm around hers. "I will watch over you, just as I did with James."

"Thank you." This woman she didn't know would one day carry her paternal line. Margaret MacLean wasn't just the chief's wife, but her ancestor, just as Mary was. She soaked in the sight of her. "It's wonderful to finally meet you."

"Aye, though likely no' under these circumstances."

"Well, one can't always pick and choose the right time for a visit, or at least so I've learnt."

"I agree." She smiled. "Tell me about yourself, Katherine. What is the world of the fae like?"

"Would you believe that they actually sent me here to you?"

"Whatever for?"

"I'm to bring about some peace between the clans."

"Oh dear." She blew out a long breath. "Then it seems you've been given an impossible task."

A knock sounded and Margaret released her. She bid the servants to enter.

Two maids and two lads hustled forward, each carrying a steaming pail of water. Maddie returned and hung a couple of gowns in the burgundy curtained ambry, while another lass carried a tray and set it on the side table.

Margaret oversaw the filling of the tub then added a few drops of scented oil. After the servants left, she shut the door and patted the chair in front of the table. "Come, Katherine. There's a warm meal. You must be hungry after your journey."

"Very, and thank you." She'd had little more than oatcakes and water for two days straight. She sat and poked her nose into the steam wafting from the bowl of chunky seafood stew. "This smells delicious." She nabbed a slice of crusty bread, dipped it, and took a hearty bite. Warmth raced to her belly. "Could you tell me exactly how you see things between the clans?"

"Of course." Margaret sat on the blue and gray padded corner chair next to her. "What do you wish to know in particular?"

"Why does Lachlan fight so hard to take possession of Islay's west?" Mary had told her Lachlan warred as he did in order to return to his clan all his father had lost, but Margaret might be able to provide more information.

"He fights to right the wrongs of his past." She dipped a finger under the red lace edging of her bodice and freed a gold necklace. The disk dangling from it held the engraved image of a unicorn. She rolled the piece between her thumb and forefinger. "In the short five years Lachlan's father was chief, he gambled away his lands on Islay, but they were unfairly lost to him. 'Tis why he's so determined to get the Rhinns back. They are his, not Angus MacDonald's."

"Do you believe the king will sort all this out now that he has all three of the feuding chiefs in Edinburgh?" She sipped wine from the goblet.

"The king wishes for my husband to enter into talks, but I know Lachlan well and he will also fight any decision the king requests if it does no' go his way." She crossed to the tub, knelt and swirled her hand through the water. "This is the perfect heat. Come and have your bath."

"I'd love one." She shed her tunic and breeches, glad to be done with the clothing she'd worn since she'd left Islay. She stepped into the tub and sank into the water. She dunked her head, emerged and picked up the soap. She lathered and worked the vanilla scented suds gently through her hair while Margaret raised her hands toward the warmth of the fire, a wistful look on her face.

Likely she bore the same expression. There was so much to think about. Margaret and Mary deserved some peace, as did their clans. Only how could she make a difference and bring about that peace without changing history?

The weight of her mission bore down on her. Gently, she picked up her amulet and squeezed it tight as the fae's words returned to her. *You and your twin are two halves of one whole, the beginning and the end. You must complete what your sister has set in motion. Keep your warrior protector close. To bring peace, you must unite.*

A chilling horn shrilled outside and Margaret hurried to the window, flung the shutters open and wedged sideways out to get a better look.

"What is it?" She splashed out of the tub, wrapped the drying cloth around her and dashed toward Margaret.

"The alert has been raised by the point watchman. An unknown vessel approaches Duart."

* * * *

John's men rowed through the dark, sending their birlinn

swiftly across the Sound of Mull toward the MacLean stronghold. Their sea crossing was almost at an end. He and Archie had followed closely in the MacLean warrior's wake, leaving only a scant few hours after their enemy had. As they rounded the point, a horn sounded with one long and eerie blast across Duart Bay.

"It appears our arrival has been noted." Archie eased onto the rear bench seat beside him and lifted the collar of his steel-studded war coat higher over his neck. "Duart Castle has never fallen for a reason. 'Tis well-guarded and impenetrable. What's your plan of attack?"

"We'll sail right into their sea-gate and request a place to rest for the night."

Archie raised a speculative brow. "An interesting plan. I take it you intend to force them into honoring the Highland code of hospitality?"

"Aye. I hardly need to raise my sword when Katherine's wish is to bring about some peace." As much as he detested having to request hospitality, he had to consider Katherine's feelings. He had to give her a fighting chance at seeing to her mission, whether he believed in it or not.

"Even if they allow us entry, they could easily slaughter us in our sleep. The MacLeans are well known for extending that form of hospitality, or have you forgotten what Lachlan so recently did to John MacIan?"

The MacIans of Ardnamurchan were their kin, and in times of war, they stood by each other's sides. When John MacIan had accepted an invitation from Lachlan to Duart Castle only a few years past, it had ended in the cold-blooded killing of eighteen of MacIan's men at Lachlan's hand, and following that, John MacIan had been locked in Duart's dungeons for a year.

"Lachlan isnae here and two of Lachlan's captains saved MacIan's life that night and stayed Lachlan's hand when he would have beheaded him. That at least gives me a little hope that not all the MacLeans are a bloodthirsty lot."

"We'll need to remain alert, to be prepared to attack if they raise arms against us." Archie leaned forward, elbows to his knees as he clasped his hands. "'Twill be an interesting night ahead."

"I have Duart in sight," Josiah bellowed from the bow, their warrior on lookout. "A guard awaits us."

"Dinnae raise your sword unless 'tis in defense." John gripped the rudder and turned them inland where the castle rose out of the misty dark with forbidding height into the night sky. "We'll be seeking the MacLeans' hospitality this eve. Although, everyone is to remain armed and prepared."

At the edge of the sea-gate, a warning shout hailed from one MacLean warrior to another then echoed up the trail to the guardsmen patrolling the barbican.

"Now, 'tis time to make it past their welcoming party." John strode to the front of the birlinn and as they neared the shore he called out to the MacLeans, "We've come at Finlay MacLean's invitation." Or close enough. "He traveled with one of our kin, and we wish to ensure Katherine MacLean arrived safely."

Four MacLean warriors waded into the water and gripped the sides of their birlinn. The head man's penetrating gaze drilled into him. "Ye'll need to await confirmation from our captain afore being permitted on our land."

A warrior with black hair and a two-handed claymore strapped to his back stormed down the trail and bounded onto the stone landing. 'Twas Arthur MacLean. He'd met him on the battlefield a year past, an adversary he'd never forget. Arthur had a strong sword arm and neither of them had been able to gain an advantage over the other.

Arthur's green eyes glinted. "Well, if it isnae John MacDonald," he bit out. "What takes you so far from your shores and brings you to Duart?"

"You have one of our kin, a woman by the name of Katherine. We seek your hospitality, and to ensure she's come to no harm during her unexpected trip."

"You can be assured she is safe and well. The chief's wife tends her." He jerked his chin toward Islay. "Feel free to leave. None here will bar your way."

"That I cannae do." He grasped the edge of the birlinn and heaved himself into the water. Surging through it, he slogged toward Arthur. "I ask that you honor the Highland code of hospitality and allow us to rest here for the night. We in turn will not raise our swords after the obvious abduction of one of our kin."

"Katherine assured me she came willingly." His gaze slid over John's men on the boat then came to rest on his brother. "Archie MacDonald. 'Tis unusual for both of Angus MacDonald's captains to leave Dunyvaig unguarded. Your trip must have been in earnest."

"After the way Katherine was taken from our land, surely you didnae expect us to sit idly by." Archie jumped into the water and splashed toward John.

"The lass is still a MacLean." Arthur rolled one sleeve and exposed the dagger sheathed at his wrist.

John hauled himself up onto the landing and planted his hands on his hips as water sluiced down his body and pooled at his feet. Gaze on Arthur, he growled under his breath. "Katherine is under my protection and until I see her with my own eyes, I willnae leave."

"You MacDonalds are a stubborn lot."

"That we are." John waited, holding steady.

Arthur narrowed his eyes then snorted. "Damn it. If I extend our Highland hospitality to you and allow your visit, then it's with the understanding your time here will be short. Your weapons will also be removed and stored in the armory."

"You cannae expect me to agree to that stipulation

considering our recent battle. Our weapons remain on us although you have my word they'll remain sheathed." This was not the time to argue, although he couldn't allow his men to go inside the enemy's walls unarmed. "A short visit suits us rather well." He extended his hand to Arthur. "Do I have your agreement?"

"Aye, but dinnae make me regret my decision." Arthur shook his hand then motioned toward the castle. "Welcome to Duart. Enter at your own peril."

"My thanks." He released a long breath then over his shoulder, called to his men, "All ashore. We've been offered Arthur MacLean's hospitality for the night."

Josiah secured their birlinn to the landing. His man and two others would remain on board for the night, guarding their only avenue of escape out.

He followed Arthur up the trail and entered the keep. In the great hall, thirty or more MacLean warriors surged around and surrounded them. No surprises there, except Highland hospitality was a sacred obligation and as Arthur hadn't been able to turn them away, so too must he respect what they'd been granted. He'd have to take great care not to overstep any boundaries, and although he'd promised only a short visit, he certainly wasn't leaving without his woman.

"I need to see Katherine MacLean." He was at Arthur's mercy with that request.

"I'm afraid she's already retired to her chamber. You will have to wait until the morn."

"I see." Hell. It grated on him to do so, but he had little choice.

Arthur offered him and his men pallets around the hearth then strode across to his warriors who'd settled down across from his men.

He'd expected naught less and would have set the same precautions in place. Near the stairwell, he chose a pallet, unraveled his plaid from over his clothing and laid down. If only he could ascend those stairs and join the woman he'd crossed the sea for. Katherine was so close yet his chest ached as if she still remained miles away. Frustration burned in his gut as he settled in the darkened corner, pulled his plaid tight around him and with his hand on his sword hilt, watched over all.

* * * *

Unbelievable. Arthur had just led John and his men through Duart's gates and into the keep, their swords still at their sides. Katherine stepped away from her window and paced her chamber. "I can't believe John's come."

Margaret closed the wooden shutters with shaky hands. "Arthur wouldnae permit the MacDonalds entry unless they requested our hospitality. Even then, I'm surprised your kin would ask such a thing considering Angus was tossed into the dungeons after requesting the same only a few short years ago. I worry whenever our clans are cloistered so closely together. Things usually never end well when that occurs."

"John's always been against my decision to travel here." She hauled on the nightrail the maid had left for her on the end of the bed. "He'll be furious he's had to step onto the enemy's land."

"Fury wouldnae drive a man to follow a woman, or request sanctuary under his enemy's roof to do so. I will go and speak to Arthur and make sure all is well." She crossed to her and gripped her hand. "Remain here. The guard outside your door will ensure you're no' disturbed throughout the night."

"Some time alone might help sort out my thoughts." She had to come up with a plan now John was here. His arrival had changed everything.

"Rest and sleep well." Margaret kissed her cheek. "We'll talk again in the morn. I wish to know more about you and your desire for peace."

"Thank you for all you've done for me tonight. It's truly

appreciated."

"You're most welcome." With a gentle smile, she closed the door behind her.

Why had John come? She climbed under the thick fur bedcover and burrowed into the soft down mattress. Heat pulsed through the room from the fire, but a chill still swept through her. She ached to go to John. The distance separating them was small but it pulled at her like the widest chasm. Only she couldn't forget he belonged to another. Damn it. This was all such a mess. Why the fae thought she could bring about peace, she had no idea.

Chapter 7

Katherine tossed and turned throughout the night. She thumped her pillow and groaned. It shouldn't be this difficult to put her impossible desire for John out of her mind. He'd agreed to a contracted marriage with another. As the hours passed, sleep continued to elude her, as did a plan.

Giving up on finding both, she shoved the bedcovers aside and nabbed one of the gowns the maid had hung in her ambry. She'd talk to John now and at least discover why he'd followed her when he'd been so insistent he'd never attempt a trip to Mull.

With the mountainous folds of rich blue fabric in hand, she eased the gown over her head. The layers slithered down her body and brushed the polished floorboards. She pulled the front laces together along the edge of the low-cut neckline, slid her feet into the matching slippers and before the looking glass, ran a brush quickly through her hair. After a pinch to her cheeks, she rolled her shoulders and inserted her resolve. She was a strong woman. She could handle one single Highland warrior.

She yanked the door open. Across the passageway, the guard straightened from a resting position against the wall and stared at her through stringy black hair. Behind him, a single candle-lit wall sconce cast an eerie glow over his leather vest studded with bits of steel.

He palmed his side sword. "'Tis a mite early to be leaving your chamber, my lady. Dawn is still some time away."

"I'd like to see my kin and it appears it can't wait. Could you take me to John MacDonald, please?"

"Aye, as you wish. This way."

She adjusted the long lace sleeves of her gown and followed him down the drafty stairwell. In the darkened great hall, the trestle tables had been moved to one side to accommodate the additional number of men sprawled across pallets. The guard motioned her toward the corner then took a position near the doors where he could survey all.

She edged toward the pallet in the shadows and knelt. John lay on his side, his dark hair a wind-tossed mess as was the growth of stubble hazing his jaw. He looked rumpled and such a sight for sore eyes.

Leaning closer, she pressed her palm against his chest and embraced the heat that reached her through his padded leather cotun. All the turmoil within her settled with that one simple touch.

"Katherine." One hushed word, filled with pain as he opened his eyes and stared at her. "Come here." Gently, he tugged her down beside him, wrapped his tartan around them both and buried his nose in her hair. "How could you leave me?"

She stroked her thumbs over his high cheekbones. "I'm sorry."

"Explain yourself." He edged up onto one elbow and gestured to Archie on the pallet at his feet to keep watch over the hall.

Archie nodded and scanned the shadowed depths of the room lit only by the light of the fire.

"Don't be mad at me," she whispered.

"I'm far beyond mad." He tucked her underneath him, lowered his mouth to hers and kissed her.

One taste was all it took to cloud her senses. She swept her hands around his neck, dragged him closer and with her heart beating frantically against his, kissed him with all the longing she'd held back since that morning they'd parted. "I've missed you, so much."

"Then dinnae leave me again." He urged her lips apart and plundered the depths of her mouth, their tongues tangling in a heated duel.

Oh, sweet heaven. She wanted more. Trailing one finger along the waistband of his pants, she encountered hard, hot skin. Skimming lower, she brushed the head of his cock straining against his leather pants for release.

"Katherine." His groan rumbled against her ear and made her tingle all over. "We need to speak, in private."

* * * *

John grasped Katherine's hands and stayed her touch. His damn cock throbbed and would spear through his trews if he didn't halt her. Kissing her, tasting the warm honey of her mouth and holding her in his arms again was a divine torture he never wanted to give up.

Across the great hall, the guard who'd escorted her downstairs remained at attention. Taking her above-stairs for their coming conversation wasn't an option, not when the guard would stop him before he'd even reached the first step. The antechamber off the hall would have to do. They needed to talk, and she needed to understand the predicament she'd placed him in. Aye, she would be leaving with him at first light, and he'd accept no other outcome. Now to make his feisty little faerie understand that's exactly what would be happening.

"Come, as quietly as you can." He stood and lifted her with him then opened the door at his back and led her into the side room. Near the window, the antechamber's bright yellow plastered wall held a silk banner embroidered with the MacLean clan crest, and under the moonlight shimmering through, eight lavishly upholstered chairs sat around a gleaming center table.

"Did you travel safely?" Katherine pushed one of the leather bound ledgers scattered on the smooth tabletop into the middle then perched on the edge.

"As well as could be considering I should never have left Islay's shores in the first place." He barred the door so they wouldn't suffer any interruption, closed the window's wooden shutters then crossed to the hearth. After kneeling on the thick woven rug of blue and green wool, he built a fire to roaring life and once the solar warmed, patted the space next to him. "Come and sit. This conversation may take some time. Are you well?"

"Yes, but tired. I only arrived here a few hours before you." She clutched her rich blue skirts and sat cross-legged in front of him. Slippers kicked off, she palmed her flushed cheeks.

"Come closer." The sprinkle of freckles across her nose made his fingers itch to trace them. He removed his sword, set it on the rug within easy reach then gripped the mat underneath her and dragged her closer when she didn't move.

"Wait." She clasped his arms.

"Nay, dinnae deny me." He seized her knees and kept her locked close. "I've missed touching you, having you in my sight. From the moment the MacLean warrior took you, I have no' been able to rest."

"Why did you come? You were so adamant you wouldn't."

"Where you are, I need to be." There was no other answer for it. "You shouldnae have run. Why did you?"

"Hearing about Madison was the last straw. It put everything into perspective for me."

"Madison who?"

"Madison MacDonald. The girl you agreed to enter into a marriage contract with."

"I did no such—" Damn. He'd forgotten all about the lass from Dunscaith. "Who told you about her?" No one other than Mary, Archie and he knew of Angus's desire for one of his captains to wed his second cousin from Skye.

"Mary did." Tears pooled in her deep blue eyes and stirred every protective emotion within him. "She told me Angus's desire was to strengthen the bonds between the two MacDonald clans. Apparently Archie gave an adamant no, but you said yes."

"Aye, although those talks disintegrated when the feud escalated and Angus was captured. The lass is barely of age."

"She's now sixteen and very much of age. Mary also said such talks are binding."

"Naught was formally contracted."

"That doesn't mean your word isn't binding." She cupped his cheek, smoothed her palm along his jaw as a tear trickled free. "Don't you see, John? She's the one you're meant to marry and spend the rest of your life with. She's the one."

"I dinnae have any feelings for her." He wiped the tear away, scooped her up and settled her in his lap. "'Tis only for you I do, and no one will keep you from me, no' even yourself. You may have come to Mull, but you willnae stay here. Your place is with me, at Dunyvaig."

"I'll never change your future. It's not right for me to do so." She pressed her chest out and the top rise of her breasts swelled against the soft blue fabric embroidered with silver thread. He traced one finger along her soft skin and over the pebbled tips of her nipples poking the cloth.

"My future is with you and was from the moment we met. What's no' right is refusing to accept that we belong together."

"Madison is the one you will marry." Adamant words, ones he wouldn't accept.

"Nay, Katherine, I willnae marry her." Aching for a closer touch, he swept the edge of her bodice to one side and filled his palm with the warm flesh of her breast. "You're the only woman who holds my heart. Without you, I cannae live. Dinnae you feel the depth of our bond? What's between us cannae be denied."

"Yes, I feel the depth, and at times to the point of pain."

She thrust her fingers into his hair and stroked his scalp.

"There is only pain when we arenae together. You cannae force me to marry another when 'tis you I need to survive." He dipped his head and grazed his teeth over her nipple. "Being apart from you these last few days has been hell. I never wish to experience such a loss again."

"But Madi—"

"Nay, enough." He took her mouth in a slow and tender kiss. "I need you as greatly as I need my next breath. You and only you."

"I need you too, but that doesn't make us being together, right."

"The fae bound us together. You are the woman I live for, the woman I wish to be joined with for all time. I want all of you, heart, body, and soul." Heat surged through his blood and he tipped her onto her back and sucked one sweet luscious nipple deep inside his mouth.

"John." She moaned and arched into him. "That feels so good."

"You are a part of me, as I long to be a part of you, and I'll do all I can to prove it." He moved to her other breast and imbibed on the tight bud. "I need to claim you as mine, to ensure you never leave my side again. 'Tis also the only way I can get you safely away from Duart. I cannae take the risk of inflaming this feud."

"But I just got here." She pressed her hand against his chest, right over his heart.

"And you shall leave again. You've crossed centuries to come to me, and when you left Islay, it near wrenched my soul in two." He was prepared to do all he must to ensure she understood the depth of his commitment. He tugged his cotun and tunic off. "I'll never allow you to remain here on MacLean land, and their hospitality ends when dawn breaks."

"I still haven't figured out what I need to do with the fae's mission. Bringing about peace without changing history isn't going to be an easy task." She shoved against his bare shoulders, rolled him onto his back and straddled his hips.

"There'll never be peace. Tell me again, word for word, exactly what the fae asked of you." This mission meant the world to her and he couldn't easily dismiss it.

She closed her eyes and said, "*You and your twin are two halves of one whole, the beginning and the end. You must complete what your sister has set in motion. Keep your warrior protector close. To bring peace, you must unite.*"

"And what exactly did your twin set in motion?"

"She had to ensure history remained on course, that Archie didn't kill Lachlan MacLean but instead placed him into the king's hands."

"And what does that have to do with coming here to Duart?"

"Nothing, but—"

"Then there must have been something else Marie set in motion that you need to complete. What else has she done?"

"I—I—" She gasped and covered her mouth. "She wed a MacDonald and joined the clans by her marriage. Oh, surely I haven't misunderstood the fae's request all this time?"

"The fae also told you to keep me close and to bring peace, we must unite. Could she possibly have meant the peace needed within my own clan, within me? I'm certainly no' at peace, no' unless we unite. A fact I intend to remedy, right now." From his tartan, he tore a strip off, clasped his right hand with her right, and wrapped his plaid around their hands. Bound together, he would ensure the peace they both sought.

"What are you doing?" She wriggled her fingers.

"'Tis a handfast. The vows we speak now will bind us together as man and wife for a year and a day, and as soon as we return to Dunyvaig, we'll be wed proper. This is the only way I'll be able to leave Duart without there being a fight. I alone am responsible for your welfare."

"The fae also said I had to wear the amulet so I was provided safe passage as I returned to my MacLean kin. Why would she ask me to journey here if I wasn't supposed to?"

"Mayhap she knew it would take all of what you and I have been through for you to recognize what is right afore your eyes. You're a MacLean, a daughter of this clan, and I'm a MacDonald. If you wed me, you'll strengthen and unite the clans exactly as you wished for."

"Goodness." A flare sparked in her eyes. "Right after the fae told me to travel to Mull she said, *If that is what it will take for you to see the truth, then that is what must be.*'"

"Aye, then do you now see the truth? You and Marie are two halves of one whole. The beginning and the end should always come full circle and your sister wed my brother. Join with me now and continue to strengthen the ties between our clans, as I wish to join with you."

"But I can't. We're in the middle of an argument." She blew out a long breath. "Getting hitched like this is all kinds of wrong."

"I promise you, we'll no' be arguing after we've spoken our vows. No' when I'll be buried deep inside you and—" Blood surged to his cock and it lengthened and stabbed her inner thigh. His trews had to go. He loosened the ties at his waist and freed his shaft.

"I can't believe this is happening." Katherine jiggled on top of him, her breasts bobbing so close to his mouth he couldn't deny himself another taste of them. "Oh," she sighed. "I really love it when you put your mouth on me like that."

"Then say aye to our joining and make it quick." He licked the peaking tips again. "I'll begin. I, John Joseph MacDonald, of Islay, pledge my troth to Katherine MacLean, of the MacLeans of Duart. With this handfast, I take her as my wife for the next year and a day." He moved to her other breast and gave it the same attention. "Speak your vow, love."

"There's still Madison to consider."

"Nay, there is no'. What does your heart tell you?"

"That joining with you always feels so right, and I'm not sure I can let you go." She heaved her skirts up and spread her folds. Gently, she held his cock and rubbed the head over her slick entrance. "I want to make us one."

"Then do it."

"You're so impossible at times." She looked deep into his eyes and smiled. "But my impossible." She slid his cock deep inside her hot channel and panting, moved up and down. "Oh, yes. You feel sooo good inside me."

"I'm still waiting to hear your vow." With a low moan, he rocked his hips. "Give yourself to me. I will love and cherish you for all of my days."

"I gave myself to you the moment I fell through the veil." She caressed his chest. "I want to feel all of your skin on mine."

Hell, her skirts were bunched between them, albeit at her waist, and he still had his trews half on. Growling, he came out of her long enough to kick his pants off and ease her gown down her legs. Rolling her over onto her back, he came up on top. His cock hammered at him to take her, and as he claimed her lips, he plunged deep inside her channel and made her his.

"Perfect." She clutched his butt and urged him to go faster. "Make me soar."

"Aye, I shall always do so." Losing himself in the woman who held his heart, he didn't hold back. He kissed her, ravishing her mouth as he pounded harder and deeper inside her. His faerie held an intoxicating allure he'd never be able to resist. She was sweet, fiery, and roused endless passion within him.

"More," she panted.

"You're so beautiful, Katherine. I want to make you come, over and over." Needing to give her everything, to hear her pleasure and have it thrum through him, he slid his hand between them. He caressed her nub then thrusting in balls-deep, took them both over the edge of no return.

"John." She gasped his name as her inner muscles tightened and dragged him home.

Giving into his own desire, he came deep inside her and with no strength remaining, collapsed on top. "Mine. You'll always be mine."

* * * *

Katherine lay on the thick rug before the hearth, John a delicious weight on top of her as the sky lightened outside the window. She stroked his back and blew gently over the light sheen of his sweat dampened skin. "John, wake up. It's almost dawn."

He eased up onto his elbows and looked into her eyes, his gaze strikingly focused. "I wasnae asleep. 'Tis impossible to find rest within the enemy's walls. Are you ready to come home?"

"I'm sorry I doubted you, and that I left without speaking to you first. The fae told me to keep my warrior protector close and to bring peace, we must unite. It's our union which is needed and I see that now with such clarity. You and Marie both raised the question about actually bringing about some peace, and yet I continually pushed your concerns aside. All I saw was the need to travel here." She threaded her bound fingers through his and smiled as the small strip of knotted cloth around their wrists tugged tighter against her flesh. "I want to speak my vow, to bind us together for all time. I just wish I didn't have to change your future to do so."

"You must have faith that the fae wouldnae have chosen wrongly for you. I hold a piece of your soul and that is meant to be." His cock twitched inside her and he rocked his hips. "Bind us together, otherwise peace will continue to elude me."

"You're also insatiable." She stroked his cheek. "But there is no one I would ever wed other than you."

"Then I shall ask you formally." He kissed her, sweeping

his tongue along hers with a slow thoroughness that made her melt. "Katherine MacLean, will you do me the great honor of becoming my wife? I wish to hold you each and every day, to love and cherish you for the rest of our lives."

"Do we get to consummate my vow once it's spoken?"

"I believe that might be possible." He glanced at where they were still joined.

The full evidence of their union hummed through her and gently, she wrapped her legs around his hips and took him deeper, feeling the stretch of tender muscles as she did and loving every moment of it. "Then yes. I'll marry you, my warrior protector."

With a deep moan, he eased out then slowly sank back in. "Hurry, love, I need to hear your vow afore I lose my mind once more."

She didn't hold back. "I, Katherine MacLean, of the MacLeans of Duart, pledge my troth to John Joseph MacDonald, the man who holds a piece of my soul. With this handfast, I take him as my husband for the next year and a day." She kissed him, her soul lifting and twining fully with his. Heat consumed her, took over her mind as every part of her fused with him. "I should have understood what the fae meant sooner. She told me I no longer belonged to the future. Even my mother told me I had to accept my place here in the past as Marie had done. I belong right here with you. Always and forever."

"Aye, always and forever, with me." He pushed even deeper, moving harder and faster with each heavenly thrust.

"You make me feel too much." She rocked forward, consumed by the scalding heat that devoured her each time they joined. Digging her fingers into his shoulders, she rode the waves of pleasure that contracted her channel and demanded he join her.

"Katherine." He pulled her harder against his cock, holding her in place as he seized her mouth and kissed her until she lost all thought.

* * * *

When her senses finally returned, Katherine stretched underneath John and breathed in his warm scent. "Mmm, I definitely feel at peace. What about you?"

"Aye, my wife, I feel at peace even though I'm within the enemy's walls." He nuzzled her neck then drew the soft skin of her flesh into his mouth and sucked.

"John." A knock sounded on the door.

"'Tis Archie," John whispered to her. "Aye, brother. I'm here," he called to him.

"Margaret is awake and asking to see Katherine. Arthur too wishes to speak with us, and our men grow restless to leave. We dinnae wish to overstay our welcome."

"We'll be out shortly."

"Good." His footsteps faded away.

John nipped her lips, eased out of her and taking her hands, helped her to her feet. "I need you to remain quiet and allow me to ensure our safe leaving. As my wife, none can keep you from me, or gainsay my decision to take you from this place."

"I understand, although you should know, I'm not really all that good at following orders." She donned her blue gown and adjusted the long sleeves over her wrists.

"Aye, as I've learnt." With a mischievous smile, he shrugged his cotun on over his white tunic, fastened his black leather trews at his waist and strapped his weapons on. "Come. We'll thank our hosts for having us then be away."

He unbarred the door then with a hand on her lower back, guided her into the crowded great hall. The trestle tables had been moved back into position and serving maids now weaved around the benches and set platters of cooked meats and bowls of hot oats on the tables. So many MacLeans filled the hall, a hundred or more warriors, their postures rigid and gazes narrowed on the trestle table holding John's men.

"I feel terrible." She burrowed closer into his side. "I didn't come here to inflame the feud."

"I know, love, but by your actions you've forced two clans to come together no long after we've battled. The MacLeans also outnumber us a dozen to one and that places them in a position of great power. 'Twould be so easy for them to sweep aside the Highland code of hospitality and have their vengeance. It has happened twice in the recent past, no' only to Angus when he tried to stem the feud, but also to one of our close kin, John MacIan from Ardnamurchan. The MacLeans will go to any means to win this war. I can only say, the sooner we're gone from here, the better."

"Katherine." Margaret called her name and motioned to her from the dais where she was seated between Arthur and Archie.

"Remain beside me at all times." He steered her toward the dais and clasped his brother's forearm. They spoke, so quietly she hadn't a chance of hearing what they said.

"Sit beside me, Katherine." Margaret shuffled closer to Arthur in her bronze skirts and made room for her. She took a seat as Archie eased across the other way and made room for John to sit next to her.

She perched on the wooden bench and squeezed Margaret's hand under the table. "Things have changed. It appears I must now go back home to Islay."

"That is for the best considering your MacDonald clan's arrival." Margaret's brows twitched nervously as she watched another dozen MacLean warriors stride into the great hall and grumble. She leaned closer, and murmured, "Eat a bite or two if you can. My clansmen need to see I've welcomed you to our table."

"Of course." She picked up the large pitcher and filled two goblets with warm cider. She passed one to John as he filled a trencher with steaming bacon, crusty bread, and sliced cheese. He nudged her to share his food. Quickly, she laid a bacon strip on top of the bread and took a bite.

Arthur, dressed in tan breeches and a forest green jerkin over a beige tunic, removed his dirk strapped to his thigh, stabbed a wedge of boiled egg from his trencher and ate it from the tip. "Do you sleep well?" he asked her.

"I'll sleep better once I return home. I'm sorry if I've caused any problems with my arrival."

"Aye, these circumstance are no' to my liking. Mayhap Finlay shouldnae have brought you to Mull."

"Your warrior, as far as we can tell, acted alone in doing so." John slid his hand under her hair and around her nape as he spoke to Arthur. "Provided we're assured safe passage from your shores, we'll hold no grudge against you and your kin for his actions. And by we, I mean my new handfast wife, myself, and my men."

"I see." Arthur lifted a brow as he twirled his dirk then speared a slice of ham from the platter. "An interesting turn of events. You should know though, that none of my men were instructed to remain on Islay after the battle, and as long as you dinnae seek to attack us, we will do naught more than protect our own borders while our chief remains in Edinburgh."

"Then we shall agree to do the same while Angus is imprisoned."

Katherine's heart lifted. Had a truce just been reached while their chiefs were in the king's hands? Perhaps her trip to Mull to seek some peace between the clans hadn't all been in vain.

"Good." John slowly stood and tugged her to her feet. "Then it appears we must leave. My thanks for your hospitality."

Archie pushed back his chair as he eyed John. "My congratulations on your handfast, brother. Your timing is impeccable."

"My congratulations too, Katherine." Margaret rose. "You'll need to fetch your things. Come, I'll help you."

"Be quick." John released her and he nodded. "I'll wait

right here.”

“I won’t be long.” She clutched Margaret’s hand and hurried upstairs.

In her chamber, Margaret nabbed her traveling bag and handed it to her. “Keep the gown. There’s no need for you to change afore you leave. At least now we’re more aware of where the MacDonald clan stands, particularly with your warrior’s promise just now to curtail any warring until his chief’s return. That’s a good sign.” A spark of hope lit her eyes. “Tell Mary I’ll be thinking of her.”

“I will. I know she thinks of you.”

A knock sounded and a MacLean guardsman wearing a darkened nasal helm, chainmail and black boots marched in. His green eyes, a paler shade than Arthur’s, glinted through the slits as he scrutinized first her then Margaret. “My lady, Hector asks for you. The boy frets when so many MacDonalds remain within our walls.”

“I’ll be but a moment.” Margaret hugged her. “Hector is my son. I must go to him.”

“Thank you for all you’ve done for me.”

“You’re welcome. Take care as you travel.” She grasped her skirts and walked from the room.

The guard shut the door, closing them in. “Now,” he grated, “’tis time for you and I to speak.”

“I too must go.” She tried to edge past him, but he blocked her way. Towering over her, he removed his helm and scrubbed a hand across his scraggly brown beard. Finlay. “What are you doing here?”

“Arthur may lead this clan in my laird’s stead, but I know Lachlan’s wishes well. He would never sit idle when we held such a bargaining chip in our hands.”

“I’ve been given safe passage to leave.”

“And you shall, with me.” He shoved a dirty wad of linen in her mouth and knotted a strip of tartan around it.

She fought, clawing at his face and kicking.

"Nay, lass." He grabbed her hands and rammed her into the wall.

Her head hit and she gagged as the room spun.

Black dots danced before her yes, and then nothing.

Chapter 8

John clenched his fists as he waited for Katherine to return. What the hell was taking her so long? His men were past ready to leave and so was he. He crossed to Arthur at the base of the stairs. "I need to collect my wife."

"She should've returned by now. I'll escort you upstairs." Arthur gestured for him to go first and he scaled the winding stairwell.

All was quiet on the second floor landing, each door leading off the darkened corridor firmly shut.

"'Tis the third door on your left," Arthur instructed.

John stopped at the door, turned the knob and strode inside. The fire had long gone out and the morning's sunshine streamed in through the window and lit the chamber with its large burgundy canopied bed and curtained ambry. A dressing screen next to the side table remained folded against the wall and next to it, Katherine's leather traveling bag had been dumped and overturned. He hunkered down and scooped it up. "She's no' here."

"She didnae pass by me." Arthur strode to the wall and wiped a smear of blood from it. "'Tis fresh."

John snarled, a low and deadly rumble. Katherine had been

taken, and not of her own free will. "What tricks do you play, Arthur?"

"None, and damn it, this has to be Finlay's doing." Arthur slammed one fist into his open palm. "He can be rash and reckless at times."

"Where will he have taken her?"

"I'll check with the guards." Arthur raced out the door and John made chase. In the great hall, Arthur ordered several of his men to begin a search.

Archie gripped John's shoulder. "What's this all about?"

"Katherine's gone, taken by Finlay." To his men, he gritted out, "We are no' at war, but I want my wife back. We'll do all we can to ensure it."

Arthur marched across to him. "Finlay was sighted leaving through the postern gate a few minutes ago, although his destination is unknown. He could be anywhere."

John sprinted out the door and his brother and men followed as he raced toward the bay. If Finlay was on the run, his options were by land or sea and he'd already proven he had a penchant for using the sea as a means of escape. He hailed Josiah and his men who'd remained on board. "Katherine is missing. Have you seen any sign of her or the warrior Finlay MacLean."

Josiah held onto the center mast and pointed toward the tip. "A nasal-helmed warrior just sailed out of the bay after carrying something bulky on board wrapped in a thick brown fur."

"That'll be them." John bounded into his boat and bellowed to his men as they followed him, "All to oars! There can be no delay. Chase the MacLean."

"We'll catch him, brother." Archie grabbed the ropes and tossed one to him as their warriors sank their oars into the waves and rowed them out of the bay.

"There were signs she struggled against her captor, Archie, and if MacLean harmed her in any way, I'll kill him." John gripped the birlinn's rope alongside his brother as the crosswind filled the sail with a hearty slap. The birlinn shot off like an arrow and his men stowed their oars.

With his feet braced wide along the side of the boat, he pulled his rope until the sail tightened. As they hit the tip, the wind blasted through and the galley rose half out of the water. He and Archie leaned farther back to counter the move and his men moved into the perfect positions to ensure their balance and that they picked up even more speed.

They skimmed the high waves, the massive square sail pulled as taut as he'd ever seen it. Ahead, the MacLean's skiff came into view along the waterway toward the south. Finlay too stood on the side of his skiff as it careened over the waves, the wind taking him swiftly toward MacLean land on Jura. "I'll lose her if he makes it to Jura's northern shore. There are too many places he could hide."

"Then we'll make sure that does no' happen," Archie shouted over the crashing of the waves.

John eyed the MacLean's skiff, his heart a pounding mess as movement stirred within the hull. Katherine shoved the fur off her head and pushed one hand out. "There she is."

The wind tore at him and the sea-spray battered his face. He'd allowed his wife to be taken from him again, and it should never have happened.

A huge wave rose and as they crested it, he gripped the rope tighter, his arms and legs burning as every muscle strained to control the wind power harnessed in the birlinn's tight sail. "Hold tight," he barked.

The bow rose sharply upward then slammed back down. The impact sent several of his warriors flying to the other side, but none were tossed overboard.

"'Tis slippery," Archie yelled as he grappled to keep his footing.

A woman's scream echoed across the raging waves as the MacLean's skiff pitched sideways and hit the icy water. A wave rolled and twisted it over. It popped bow up and sank. Gone, swallowed whole, and by the same rogue wave that had almost toppled them.

John's heart stopped beating. He tossed Josiah his rope, tore off his cotun and weapons as his brother did the same.

He dove into the frigid water and allowed the raging waves to close over him as he kicked downward into the murky depths.

* * * *

Katherine's head shattered with pain as icy, turbulent waters surged and dragged her under. She'd barely come to when Finlay had roared the skiff was going down. The crashing waves tossed her about. So deep.

The fur bedcover, still half wrapped around her, tore at her chest and legs. She wrenched it free and it jerked away into the swirling vortex of nothingness. She yanked out the gag and black hazed her vision. No. Clawing with all her might, she fought toward the surface. The sea wouldn't take her, not now she'd finally found the man who was hers. She had to get back to John.

An arm cinched around her waist.

She lurched around and stared into the most piercing golden eyes. John firmed his hold on her and pushed them upward through the twisting current, and in a flurry of bubbles, they broke the surface.

"J-John?" She gulped in great drafts of air. "Is it really you?"

"'Tis I. You were down so deep." He cupped the back of her head and drew her closer. His dark hair floated around his neck as he treaded water for them both.

He was real, his body solid, his flesh warm and his hold tight. She clutched his shirtfront as over his shoulder, a birlinn bobbed on the water. Cheers erupted from his men on board and a few others in the water surrounding her. "F-Finlay came to my chamber."

"I know, love. I made chase as soon as I could." He swept

her hair back from her forehead and touched a spot that throbbed. "You've got a nasty gash that needs tending."

"You're not hurt are you?"

"Nay, no' a scratch. Let's get you out of this cold water." He cut a fast path through the churning waves toward the birlinn, gripped her waist and boosted her upward.

Josiah reached, grasped her hands and lifted her up. Another man smothered her in a thick MacDonald tartan and then John was there, sopping wet as he scooped her up and carried her to the stern. He sat on the wooden bench and cradled her on his lap, his fingers biting into her sides. He shook, whether from anger or fear, she wasn't sure.

"It's all right." She wound her arms around his neck and plastered herself against him. "Where's Finlay? And where exactly are we?"

"Off the coast between Mull and Jura." He glanced at Archie as he hauled himself into the birlinn.

"Heave," Archie called to one of his men in the water. He reached over the side and grunting, lugged a body on board. Water sluiced from the hefty chainmail wrapped around Finlay and his head lolled back on an impossible angle. Two men carried his body to the bow and beyond her sight. Archie strode toward her and knelt at her feet. "Did you suffer any injuries?"

"What happened to Finlay?"

"There was naught I could do. He broke his neck in the fall." Ever so gently, he lifted her hair from her forehead and muttered under his breath. "Damn him. He hurt you."

"Are you sure Finlay's dead?" She shivered uncontrollably.

"Aye, we'll bury him on Jura. For now, we'll set sail afore any more MacLeans have the chance to catch us up." He strode away.

"No one is supposed to die because of me." She grasped John's shirtfront.

"His death was a surety the moment he stole you away.

What happened to him isnae your fault." John tore a strip from his tunic's hem, wrapped it around her head wound and knotted it lightly.

Hot tears burned behind her eyes.

"Katherine, nay." John tipped up her chin. "Look at me. You're no' to blame yourself for his death."

"I've changed history. He isn't supposed to die because of me." She tucked her cheek on his chest and shivered inside the tartan.

"A warrior's life is never long and he chose his own destiny." He tucked her drying hair behind her ear. "Rest while we sail. I'll watch over you."

"Don't stop talking to me." Her eyelids drooped. All that had happened over the past few days caught up with her and darkness edged her vision. "I need to hear your voice."

"You need to rest more than…"

She battled to focus on his drifting voice. He was all she'd ever dreamed of, and now safe again in his arms, she let go and allowed the dark to pull her under.

* * * *

Waves slapped against the birlinn's sides as the boat rocked and dipped, the sound tugging Katherine further toward wakefulness.

"Go back to sleep." John's voice floated over her then his lips brushed her cheek. "Sleep."

She stretched and pushed her eyes open. Night had fallen and the moon, hidden behind a dark layer of cloud, cast John's face in shadow. "Where are we?"

"We've no' long left the northern tip of Jura. Archie brought the birlinn into shore and buried Finlay on MacLean soil. The wind is easing now, so we'll need to make landfall somewhere safe for the night. You've naught to fear. We'll soon pass from MacLean land to our MacDonald soil. You'll be safe."

"I'm always safe when I'm with you." She cupped his

stubbly jaw. "I'm not sure I ever thanked you for coming to my rescue."

"I gave you my promise of protection and 'twill always stand firm."

"So I've learnt." She edged up and kissed his chin.

"You're such a complete distraction." His gaze held deep longing and it pulled at her heart. "Kiss me again, my sweet imp, and this time dinnae miss my lips."

"And you're a demanding man, but I love that." She licked his lower lip and as he groaned, she grinned. "I've heard distraction is good for the soul."

"So is a little peace."

"Well, you know me. I'm all for a little peace."

Chapter 9

As the wind died away, the men lowered the sail and rowed. They passed into the southern portion of Jura's waters and after rounding the tip, cruised into an isolated bay. Beside Katherine, John lifted his face to the night sky, his eyes closed as he breathed deep. She did the same, taking in the scents of salty sea and Scotland's freshest air. She was home, or at least now very close to home.

Ahead, along the rugged and untouched coastline, moonlight bathed the woodland's treetops a silvery hue. "This is such a beautiful place."

"Aye, and the place where we'll rest for the night."

They came ashore and the men set up camp, hunted game then roasted their meal over an open fire. Her belly rumbled as the succulent aroma of cooked goose pervaded the air.

She sat close to the fire on the blanket John spread out, her knees snuggled to her chest as the fire's brilliant orange and red flames warmed her through. Her gown was almost dry, although the salt encrusted fabric irritated and made her want to scratch her itchy skin.

"Are you all right?" John settled in behind her, his legs either side of hers.

"I could really use a wash and a change of clothes."

"There's a loch no' far from here. We'll bathe after we've eaten." He tugged her back until she rested against his chest. Gently, he twined a lock of her hair around his finger, his warmth fully enclosing her. "You have the most beautiful hair. 'Tis so pale it shimmers like gold."

"It does?"

"Aye," he purred in her ear, "and I want to see it lying across my pillow, each and every night." He selected one of the sticks of meat from the fire, tore off a chunk and slipped the morsel between her lips.

"That could be arranged, provided we ever see a bed." She plucked a piece of meat from the skewer and fed him.

In silence, they ate as the other warriors did the same. A few men remained close to the fire while half a dozen others strolled down to the water's edge and washed up. These men were islanders and seafarers. They lived and breathed the sea and were most content when closest to it.

Archie bounded from the beached birlinn, a couple of bags in hand and his tartan slung over his shoulder. He set one of the bags at his feet and passed the other to John. "That's yours."

"My thanks." John placed it behind him.

Archie chose a skewer then perched on a low boulder and glanced at her. "How do you fare?"

"Much better. I want to thank you for coming to Mull for me too. I never meant to cause such trouble."

"You're my sister-by-marriage, and with your handfast to my brother, now my sister twice over. I will always be here for you."

John slid her hair over her shoulder and dropped a soft kiss on her neck. "We're your kin, more so than the MacLeans will ever be. Which means there'll be no more traveling to Mull."

"Now, that I can promise you. I'm content to remain on Islay with you, although"—she shuffled around and faced him—

"do you think there's a way to get a message to Margaret, to let her know I'm all right? I'm certain she'll worry."

"I cannae give you any promises, but if the opportunity ever arises, I'll send word. Have you eaten your full?"

"Yes."

"Then let's bathe." John gripped her waist and set her on her feet as he stood then nabbed his bag.

She flapped out the tartan blanket they'd sat on, and with it wrapped around her for added warmth, followed him into the moonlit recesses of the forest.

John prowled ahead, keeping an eye out along the densely wooded trail. He strode with such purpose, his leather pants clinging to his powerful thighs and molding his tight butt. He was so delectably gorgeous with his white tunic fluttering free. A gentle breeze whispered through the trees, lifted his shirt hem and gave glimpses of his golden skin lit by the moonlight. "We're here." He held up a low branch and she passed under it.

"Oh, this is beautiful." The loch, small, private and perfectly round was encircled with towering trees and its dark, glassy surface, beckoned her to come and swim. "How did you know this loch was here?"

"When we need to make landfall, this cove is a favored place to make camp." He unwrapped her blanket from around her then laid it on the ground under a tree. "Do you need aid with removing your gown?"

"No, not since the ties fasten in front, but still I'd love your help." She removed her slippers and stepped up to him.

"This is one task I'm always up for." He picked up the front ties and unlaced her stays, his warm breath feathering across every inch of skin he exposed. Slowly, gently, he slid his hands under the fabric covering her shoulders, eased the garment down her arms and skimmed it over her hips. The crinkly blue velvet swished into a puddle at her feet and exposed all of her. "Now, this is beautiful."

"Are you coming in with me?" She backed up a step and his hungry golden gaze sent tingles racing across her skin and heat pooling in her below.

"There is no' a soul who could stop me." He divested himself of his weapons, a sword and sheathed wrist and ankle daggers, then lifted his tunic over his head. Chest muscles flexed and rippled as he shucked off his boots and pants. As he stepped forward, his silky dark hair wisped with blond slid sensuously over his broad shoulders.

She could watch him forever, exactly like this. Every inch of him was hers, and she longed to join with him.

"What are thinking?" He scooped her into his arms and walked toward the mossy edge of the loch. As his erect shaft grazed her bottom, her nipples beaded tight.

"That I'll have to insist on more than just bathing. Are you up for a little adventure?"

"Always." He strode into the water and when it lapped at his waist, he slowly lowered.

She gasped at the shock of cold and clamped her hands around his neck. Down they went and under the surface. She released him and came back up, water streaming through her hair and over her breasts. "Oh goodness. You could have warned me you were about to do that."

"Aye, although you're the one who just requested a little adventure. I was simply supplying it." He leaned in and kissed her, taking her breath away a second time with the heat of his mouth on hers.

"Then did I mention I also like to play?" She shoved a wave of water at him and backed away. "Catch me if you can." She ducked her head and dove. Kicking toward the center of the pool, she remained below, although not for long. He snaked an arm around her waist and hauled her to the surface far sooner than she'd thought possible. She dragged in a deep breath. "I see it'll take quite a bit to catch you off your guard."

"More so now than ever afore." He pressed his powerful body against hers, their legs entwined and his cock nudging her entrance.

Her heart beat frantically at having him so close, and the desire-filled look in his eyes, made her nipples tighten and throb. She ached for his mouth on them. "Come inside me."

"Aye, I long to. Soon. I wish to love all of you first." He lowered his head and kissed her, his lips so warm and silky soft, then with the smoothest of caresses, he licked across her tongue and fired all her senses.

She encircled her arms around his neck, wrapped her legs around his waist and ravished his mouth as he ravished hers.

"Your passion inflames my own, Katherine." He carried her toward the loch's mossy edge and lifted her up. Cool air washed over her body as he laid her shoulders back on the spongy surface, her bottom still in the water. Gently, he cupped one breast and rubbed the tip until the peak hardened even further. "You have the sweetest, pinkest nipples. I dream of devouring them at night."

"Kiss them." She pressed her breasts together. "I love feeling your mouth on my body, all of my body."

He held her gaze as he lowered his head and lapped her nipples. The hot stroke of his tongue sent shards of pleasure rippling through her. "Like so?"

"Exactly like so." Arching into his mouth, she drowned in the storm of sensations. Then he raised her legs, hooked them over his shoulders until her bottom lifted out of the water and fully exposed her to him.

"Ah, you also have the sweetest, pinkest flesh below too. So lush, and just waiting for me to taste." He plunged two fingers deep inside her and pumped as he captured her clit between his lips. The dual attack had her crying out. She bucked as pleasure swept through her.

She was going to lose her mind, but before she did, she'd

make certain he lost his right along with her. Under the water, she searched and found his cock and with her fingers wrapped around his thick shaft, she worked him in long pulls.

"Katherine." He groaned her name. "I love how you touch me." He circled his fingers inside her and as an explosion of heat swirled, her orgasm built, hard and sharp.

"John, inside me. Now. I can't wait any longer." She whimpered and writhed against him.

"Aye, now." He released her legs, lifted her against him and filled her in one deeply penetrating move. Then he took her over, driving her toward the edge as he thrust in a wild and raw beat.

Unable to hold on, she came apart, her inner muscles dragging and throbbing around him. Blissful spasm after spasm shook her body as she held him to her. He was her Highlander, the warrior she'd traveled through time for, and the man who'd forever be hers.

* * * *

John was lost as Katherine's hot channel pulsed around him. He roared, his release exploding violently along with hers as he spilled his seed deep within her.

Theirs was a miraculous union, his soul interlocking so tightly with hers they'd never be separated. "My wife," he whispered against her lips. "You hold my heart in your hands."

Tears misted her gaze. "And you hold my soul in yours."

"As I always will." They'd be together until the very end, and he'd make certain of it.

Cradling her in his arms, he waited as his breathing settled and his pulse slowed. Gently, he carried her out of the water and laid her down on the tartan blanket, and throughout what remained of the night, he lavished more attention on every single inch of her.

'Twas the most enchanting night as he learned her body and what brought her the ultimate pleasure, and even though the first rays of dawn stole it from him, it would only be the first of many.

At dawn's break, they rose and dressed.

Katherine donned one of his spare tunics and a pair of his breeches and though the pants were too big, she secured the soft cotton around her hips with a belt. The sight of her in his clothing stirred him, had him itching to undress her and take her all over again. Thank heavens the fae had bound her to him. He would have a lifetime to love her and he didn't want to miss a moment of it.

After packing her gown away in his bag, she eyed him. "That's one intriguing look on your face. What are you thinking?"

"That I adore the fae." He tucked his shirttails into his leather trews and strapped his sword belt and weapons on.

"They're a mischievous bunch, and I once heard from a very reliable source, that they like to tinker and play." She passed him the bag and shook out their blanket.

"As well as provide missions."

"I'm not sure I'm up for any more missions."

"You'll need to be. I have one of my own for you." He ran his fingers through her silky white-blond hair and tidied her waist length locks as best as he could. "One I intend for us to undertake together."

A mission that included their vows being spoken before a clergyman this day. 'Twas time to live his life with the woman of his dreams, and with her tucked under his shoulder, he returned, boarded their birlinn and set sail for Dunyvaig.

Aye, she was his woman. His faerie.

He'd keep her safe, and never let her go.

Chapter 10

Inside the hot, steamy recesses of their underground cavern the day following their marriage ceremony, Katherine lay sprawled across John's chest on the small curve of sandy beach as water lapped her toes. Filled with happiness, more than she'd ever known in her life, she played her fingers through the soft smattering of dark hair on his chest. "I never imagined my death would lead to living my life like this."

"You're alive and you must no' think otherwise." He smiled, caressed down her bare back and cupped her bottom. "And if I need to prove that to you every day, I shall."

"Yes, please. Prove away."

"I love you." He rolled her over and still joined as one from their recent lovemaking, stroked deeper into her slick heat. "We'll live a long life, together. I promise you that."

"I love you too." Her heart lifted and she clasped the amulet at her neck. "You're my warrior protector, and I belong right here with you, always and forever."

"Aye, as you promised me in your vows." He kissed her, so deeply the heat in her blood surged.

"Make me fly," she whispered against his lips.

With breathtaking speed, he did just that, until they soared beyond their bodies. Their love transcended both the future and the past, was built from the depths of their souls to the heights of their hearts.

Oh yes, her future was now hers for the taking, and it would be an adventure she'd never let go of.

Her greatest mission was about to begin.

To be bound to her warrior protector, for all time.

Heart, body, and soul.

Author's Note

After I wrote Highlander's Magic featuring Marie and Archie, I longed to write Katherine and John's story. I'm so glad I finally got the chance to share their tale with you.

The ruins of Dunyvaig Castle holds such history within its crumbled stone walls, along with a past I find completely fascinating. With the rich accounts told of the Highlander clans who lived in the Western Isles, I'm driven to keep what I can of the past alive. So within my *Highlander Heat* series expect history mixed with fantasy and adventure as I weave stories around actual events and people who lived at the time.

For the purposes of this story, I chose to send Katherine MacLean back to the year fifteen-hundred and ninety, because Angus MacDonald, the eighth Chief of Clan MacDonald of Dunnyveg had been imprisoned by the king due to his feud with the MacLean of Duart, his brother-in-law. The king did in fact induce all those involved in the dispute, being Donald MacDonald of Sleat, Angus MacDonald of Dunnyveg and Lachlan MacLean of Duart, to go to Edinburgh. When they each arrived, they were apprehended and imprisoned.

In the other stand-alone books in this *Highlander Heat* series, you can catch the individual stories of the clans, and discover how the feud began and the ramifications of it as it raged.

Angus MacDonald's successor was his son James MacDonald, a minor, and with someone needing to lead the clan, I chose John and his brother, Archie.

John MacDonald and Katherine MacLean however are fictional characters.

The faerie circle and the amulet bestowed to Katherine's sister, along with its passage down through Mary MacDonald's maternal line were also my addition to the story.

Although the account told by John, of Donald MacDonald and his men seeking shelter on the MacLean's portion of Jura, as well as James being taken hostage, Angus's release and his meeting with MacLean at Mullintrea, are as accurate as I could convey them from the historical information on record of this event. Following this tragedy, the feud continued to rage and all within the Western Isles were affected. Ravaging by fire and sword, both MacDonald and MacLean laid waste to huge portions of land.

This story is woven with as much accuracy to the period and locations as possible, but any mistakes made are mine alone.

This book forms part of my *Highlander Heat* series, and each within it are stand-alone.

Please feel free to search for any of my other works. I simply adore strong heroines, and have a ton of fun matching them with their honorable alpha heroes.

Also available in paperback
Scottish Historical Romance

Traveling through time…for a Highlander.

Highlander Heat Series

Highlander's Castle, Book One

Highlander's Magic, Book Two

Highlander's Charm, Book Three

Highlander's Guardian, Book Four

Highlander's Faerie, Book Five

Highlander's Champion, Book Six

by Joanne Wadsworth

Looking for more sexy Scottish adventure?

Read on to catch a preview of the next book in the
Highlander Heat series.

Highlander's Champion

Highlander Heat Book Six

by Joanne Wadsworth

Highlander's Champion

Highlander Heat Series, Book Six

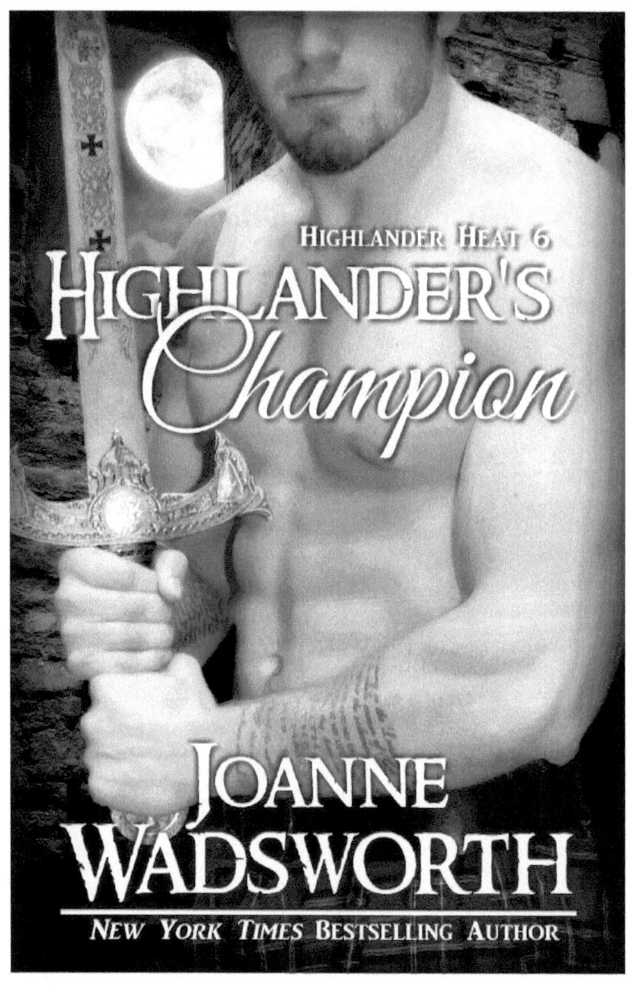

Samuel Cunningham

The battlefield on the Isle of Lewis, Scotland, 1569.

As the cold of night fully descended, Samuel Cunningham stood amongst the MacLeod of Dunvegan's warriors within the forest bordering a field swirling with tendrils of fog. Their enemy awaited them on the other side, a good hundred MacKenzie warriors in battle attire, their torches lit and staked into the ground.

Tormod, the Chief of MacLeod, stormed back and forth before his captains, fury riding him hard. "'Tis time to take the castle of Stornoway back. This is our kin's MacLeod land and no invaders will steal it. Samuel, you're to lead our right wing, John, the left, and the remainder of us will hold the center. We hit them hard, advancing as one once the hour of truce has passed." He halted and eyed Anna MacLeod, their healer and the mother of Samuel's betrothed, Zenia. "Anna, you're to return to camp with one of my guardsmen. I willnae have you caught up in the middle of this battle."

"You need every warrior at your side, Chief. I can make my own way back," she pleaded.

"Nay, Anna. I gave Zenia my word no harm would come to

you. Your daughter needs—"

A thundering roar reverberated as the MacKenzies plowed across the battlefield, breaking the truce well before its time.

"All to arms." Tormod shoved his sword high in the air and bellowed, "We fight, for justice and freedom. Let us take these blackguards down."

Samuel raced through the underbrush along the line of MacLeod warriors to the right, hauled his claymore from his scabbard across his back and released a bloodcurdling battle cry. He and the right wing rushed forward and into the fray of fierce MacKenzies.

He swung and fought, sweat pouring from his body just as his clansmen did the same. In the dark, the sound of men grunting and fighting echoed all around. They had to win this war. They fought not only for their MacLeod kin here on Lewis, but also to keep their enemy from bringing their war to Dunvegan's shores. He'd never allow any harm to come to the woman he loved, the woman he intended to wed the moment he returned to her.

He slashed toward the center, inching closer toward Tormod.

"Be prepared to die." A warrior came at him and Samuel blocked the MacKenzie's swift blow. Their claymores clashed dead center, steel ringing loud against steel. Another MacKenzie swung and struck Samuel's ribs. Pain ricocheted through him and he staggered back from the brutal blow. Two against one. Damn bloodthirsty MacKenzies. They fought dirty.

Breath ragged, he collapsed to his knees. Blood covered the padded armor of his steel-studded war coat, the blood of the warriors he'd slain now mingling with his own. He clutched his side and tried to stem the flow but his life-force poured through his fingers.

"Samuel!" A woman's cry rang out and Anna hurried from the darkened tree tine clutching her brown woolen kirtle's skirts.

"Nay, stay back, Anna," he rasped and spat out a mouthful of blood. The metallic taste coated his tongue and pervaded the air. She should've returned to camp.

"Where are you hurt?" She fell to her knees in front of him, her long red-gold locks, the same beautiful shade as Zenia's, bundled under a woolen cap.

"My side. There's naught you can do." He tried to heave to his feet but fell and slumped onto his back.

Anna shoved his war coat up and gasped. "You must live, Samuel. Zenia needs you." She glanced across the field littered with bodies and warring men, "Tormod. Hurry, come. I cannae heal this."

Tormod struck the MacKenzie he fought with one brutal blow of his blade then sprang over the fallen to Samuel's side. He dropped to one knee and grasped his forearm. "Hold fast, Samuel."

"I cannae leave Zenia." The chilly air invaded his limbs.

"I'll do what I can." Tormod raised his hands and called forth his great gifted skill. "With the power of my ancestral MacLeod fairy blood, I wish for a portal to open. Allow Samuel to seek the light and journey to where he shall find peace and aid. Send him swiftly on his way and return him again one day."

A fierce wind whipped around Samuel and a swirling vortex opened.

Anna scampered backward in the slick grass and knocked into a slain MacKenzie. The enemy's breath rattled in his chest, blood coating his face and obscuring his eyes as he lifted one fisted hand. A dagger gleamed in the moonlight then he plunged his weapon down and Anna screamed.

"Nay!" Samuel heaved up but fell away into the churning dark abyss. It took him, heart, body, and soul.

Arianna's Arrival

Seventeen years later, approaching the bridge over the Cairn Water, near Glencairn Castle, Scotland, 1586.

Death pervaded this place where murder had struck. Zenia MacLeod crouched and pressed her palm against the gritty soil lining the old carriage route bordered with lime trees. The earth shook and the wind rustled the fallen autumn leaves into a swirling mass of reds and burnt oranges. 'Twas midday yet the skies overhead darkened as if night were about to fall.

Eyes closed, Zenia reached out with her healer's senses and searched. The souls that had recently passed in this place still lingered with nowhere to go and their desperate call for help ricocheted deep inside her. Some might brand her a witch, but her soul glowed with light, her gifted skill used only to help those who asked for her aid and these lost souls did.

Standing, she raised her hands and called forth her skill. "With the power of my ancestral MacLeod fairy blood, I wish for a portal to open. Free these displaced souls in need of aid and allow them to seek the light."

The wind whistled through and whipped her blue skirts about her legs. Stars shimmered all around and those lost souls in need streaked toward the light and through the portal.

To further aid them on their way, she made another wish. "May your journey take you to where your light shines brightest and you long to be. Find the peace you seek."

The portal's swirling vortex began to close then slowed as a blazing star streaked through. The star crashed into the bushes along the roadside as the portal shimmered shut. This had never happened before. She hurried to the scrub and knelt as the bright light dispersed. A lass of mayhap seven and ten, her long golden blond tresses crackling with energy lay sprawled within the springy leaves of brushwood. She remained motionless, not a breath escaping her, then she gasped, her chest suddenly rising and falling as she slumped to her side once more.

Zenia fluttered her hand close to the lass's mouth and her breath warmed her palm. The girl lived, although strange clothing clung to her body, the shiny white fabric holding strands of gold woven within. She plucked the shiny thread which stretched then rebounded back onto her. Unusual, although no matter where the lass had come from, she clearly needed her aid. Zenia set to work and examined her for injury. Her knees and elbows were covered in grit and her right leg and arm, bent at a terrible angle, would cause her great pain when she realigned her limbs. 'Twas just as well the girl remained unaware.

"I saw bright lights!" a warrior called as he rode across the bridge, his shoulder-length locks of auburn brushing the massive two-handed claymore holstered to his back. He pulled his horse to a halt and jumped down. "Is someone hurt?"

"This lass here is injured."

"Where did she come from? She seemed to appear from the lights."

"She did, and she came through a portal I open—" She shouldn't speak so freely. He wasn't one of her clansmen who'd seen her skill rise when she called it forth, except a sense of trust shimmered through her and it was strong.

"I hold only respect for the gifted." The warrior eyed her. "There's naught to fear from me. You said you opened a portal?"

She gave into her instinct, and said, "Aye, 'twas a portal she came through. I'm Zenia MacLeod." She stroked the lass's long blond locks back from her face as a surge of protectiveness rose. "She needs aid and I must do all I can to help her."

"Who is she?"

"I've no idea." She untangled the girl's hair from around a silver chain at her neck and lifted a charm free. Engraved upon the disk was an image of the unicorn, the same mythical creature that graced her own paternal Cunningham clan crest. She turned the charm over and smoothed her thumb over the words etched upon the back.

Arianna MacLeod Cunningham.
DOB: 1998.

"Her name is Arianna."

The warrior knelt next to her in his black leather trews and tan padded cotun and inspected the inscription. "It says her date of birth is the year nineteen ninety-eight. That cannae be right."

"Aye, 'tis of a time over four-hundred years from now."

"She isnae dressed like any lass I've seen." He frowned. "Although, I've heard tales of a skill like yours. It runs deep through your MacLeod line, no' that I've ever met one of your kin who has it."

"'Tis a rare ability and I only speak of it amongst my closest, or those I sense I can trust."

"What happened here to cause you to open a portal?"

"There were so many who'd recently passed and I heard their call for aid. When I opened the portal, they flew toward the light, although I've never had one of flesh and blood arrive. She's the first to ever travel to me." She grasped his hand. "Please, you cannae speak of this to another. No' all understand as you do."

"You have my word I'll keep your secret. I would never bring harm to one so gifted." He turned his gaze on the lass and gently cupped her cheek. "She's alive and now in need of aid. I'll gladly do all I can."

"Then she has come to the right place, where her soul desired and her light shines brightest. I thank you for your offer and will gladly accept your help." She covered his hand with hers and looking deep inside her mind, searched to ensure he was all he'd proclaimed to be. Aye, his strength was undeniable, and he held great honor. That knowledge satisfied her. "Your name, kind sir?"

"James MacDonald, from clan MacDonald on the Isle of Skye."

"You are a long way from home."

"Aye, I'm traveling to Edinburgh and sailed by way of the Firth of Clyde. My chief has sent me on his behalf to speak to the king." He swayed, planted both hands on the ground and squeezed his eyes shut. "I see something, a vision. Do you see it?"

A vision shimmered to life and she closed her eyes and embraced what was to come.

The girl before them raced out of a tall building, one not made of stone, but instead built of metal and glass. Arianna glanced back at the sign above the building. The wooden plaque proudly displayed the name *Isle of Skye Dance Studio*. Giggling, she twirled a pair of dainty white slippers in her hand as she stepped onto a thoroughfare of stony black. The path wasn't one that conveyed horse and cart but machines made of steel with wheels. One slammed into Arianna and she flew over the top and landed in a crumpled heap. As the machine screeched to a halt, the lass's form flickered and disappeared. Gone. And now she was here in the past.

Zenia opened her eyes as the warrior did the same. "My

apologies. Somehow I connected the three of us when I touched you and you saw her plight as I did."

"She most certainly comes from the future." He shook his head and blinked. "What I saw was far beyond this place. A large contraption on wheels hit her. Do you experience such visions often?"

"From time to time. She's clearly a lost soul, and her charm tells me she is of both clans, MacLeod and Cunningham, just as I am." She touched her chest. As blood of her blood, she would watch over the lass sent to her. "I'm the healer of clan Cunningham. I live in a cottage in these woods near the Earl of Glencairn's residence, and I need to remain with her. If you would, could you please follow the stream a furlong or two along the forest trail until you reach my cottage then bring me the basket of healing herbs and supplies sitting beside my front door?"

"Aye, I'll be as quick as I can." He bounded onto his black destrier and urged his mount between the trees either side of the thickly forested path.

Thanks heavens she would have this warrior's aid. She shoved her long red-gold locks over her shoulder and collected some sturdy sticks of just the right length. She tore a piece of cloth from the hem of her blue woolen kirtle and as carefully as she could, realigned Arianna's arm and leg. She bound the girl's limbs in place with the sticks and cloth, just as her mother, Anna, had taught her so many years ago.

The warrior returned and rode to her side, jumped down and looped his horse's reins over a low branch. "I have what you asked for." He set her basket on the ground and cupped the girl's cheek. "She's warm and still lives."

"Aye. She is strong even though injured." She cleaned the girl's scrapes and wounds, applied a salve to keep her clear from any infection then directed James to carry Arianna's limp body back to her home.

The child would heal and survive.
She'd make certain of it.

Clan Cunningham

Two months later, at Glencairn Castle, the residence of the seventh Earl of Glencairn.

Zenia folded her hands in her lap as she sat in the earl's solar.

"Why have you come to me, Zenia?" Cunningham eased back in his chair before the grandly carved desk the old earl had sat behind.

"When I came to you after my mother's death, you offered me sanctuary and ensured I had a home and for that I am most grateful."

"My clan needed a healer and you have served us well over the years. I had no doubt you would after coming to us from the Chief of MacLeod's home. Is this visit about the lass you healed who came through one of your portals?"

"William told you?"

"Aye. He mistook her at first for one of his own sisters, which I find hard to believe."

William, the earl's eldest son, was a strong warrior who excelled with the sword. He'd come across Arianna the week before in the woods as she'd taken a walk. Each day she'd gained more strength and when William had returned with Arianna to her cottage, the three of them had spoken of all that had happened. Zenia had naught to hide from her own clansmen, and she'd known then it would only be a matter of time before she spoke to the earl about Arianna.

"William did mistake her. She is almost identical to the twins, and so too is she ten and seven as your daughters are." Arianna deserved all she could possibly provide for her, which was why she was here. "The lass is kin to me, just as she is kin to you. Her name is Arianna MacLeod Cunningham."

"So William told me, and that she hails from the Cunninghams on the Isle of Skye, your place of birth." He rested his elbows on his desktop and tapped his fingertips together. "What is it about her that convinces both you and William she comes from the future?"

"You need only speak to her yourself to see the truth." She cleared her throat. "Excuse me. I didnae mean to be so forthright."

"'Tis fine." His steely-gray gaze narrowed. "William also tells me there's a MacDonald warrior on my land. The two of them fought."

"James MacDonald was passing through on his way to Edinburgh and witnessed Arianna's arrival. He aids me as he can but must soon continue on with his travels. His trip has been delayed by several weeks and his chief awaits his return on Skye after he visits with the king." She fidgeted with the pleats in her forest green skirts. The Cunninghams and the MacDonalds rarely got along. "James gave the lass his offer of protection, and she is such a delight."

"You've become attached to the child?"

"Aye. She also enjoys learning my craft and is a natural with the healing herbs. I'm here this day because I have a request."

"Then speak freely, Zenia." The morning sun broke through

the thick layer of cloud outside and filtered through the window. It played over the papers and the pile of seneschal's accounts set neatly to the side of the earl's desk.

"Arianna needs a home such as yours. I cannae provide for her all she will need."

"You wish for me to bring her into my household? My, my." He leaned back, his chair creaking as he did. "That is a bold request."

"She has incredible knowledge to offer. She also left behind a father she loved. She has no one and I brought her into this time and have been unable to return her. I've tried, so many times, but my ability to open a portal only rises for those souls who've already passed, or those who hover on the edge of death as she did. I fear she is here to stay."

"Even as bold as your request is, I am intrigued." He tapped the polished oak desktop. "I would need to meet her afore I could make a decision."

"Most certainly." Hope bloomed in her chest. "She awaits outside."

"Then by all means, bring her in."

She dashed to the thickly paneled door and opened it. Arianna stood in the darkened hallway in a simple gown of brown, one she'd embroidered for her along the ruffled neckline with gold thread to match her long golden locks.

"Is all well?" Her big blue eyes asked so much more.

"Come in, my dear. The earl will see you." She squeezed Arianna's hands then motioned her through.

Arianna entered and dipped her head at Cunningham. "It's lovely to meet you, my laird."

"Hell." He shoved to his feet and yanked on the front of his gray tailored jacket. "You are as I've been told. I can barely tell the difference between you and my daughters."

"The man at your door got quite the surprise when I arrived." Arianna shuffled from slippered foot to foot on the burgundy woolen mat before his desk.

"Take a seat and tell me all about this time in the future you're from. Your speech certainly isnae as thick as mine."

"I was born in the year nineteen ninety-eight and lived on the Isle of Skye with my father." She sat on one of the three navy and black striped padded chairs set in a half circle. "He fashions weapons of old and sells them all around the world, or will, in the future. His name is Samuel Cunningham. He's all I have."

Zenia had been quite shocked when Arianna had first spoken her father's name, although her surprise had quickly passed. Samuel was a common name, and so was Cunningham. The child's kin also came from Skye where names were more often than not handed down from generation to generation.

"There are a number of Cunninghams on Skye, all from my clan. Tell me about the future." Eagerly, he walked around his desk, moved his quill and ink bottle and perched on the front edge.

"In the future all children attend school from a very early age, both girls and boys alike. I just completed my final year of secondary school and recently enrolled at the University of West Scotland to further my studies."

"You're well educated?"

"Very well educated."

"What of your mother?"

"I never knew her, although I bear her name. She too was called Arianna and was a MacLeod. She died not long after I was born and Dad's been fighting an illness called cancer these past few months."

"Is this illness one he might perish from?"

"If he'd discovered his illness a little earlier, he could have easily caught it in time. His chances right now are half and half." Tears welled in her eyes and she blinked them away. "I've written him a letter, one I need you to hold onto and ensure he receives in the future. His address is on the outside and the date it must be delivered to him by. I've warned him about his cancer and told him as much as I could." She pulled a piece of parchment folded in three from her pocket and handed it to the earl. "Will you keep it safe for me and ensure he receives it?"

"Aye, I'll do all I can, but you're asking me to ensure he receives this in a time over four-hundred years from now." He took her letter and inspected the address on the outside. "He lives in Dunvegan Village?"

"A few miles north of it, yes. Our home is close to Dunvegan Castle, right along the cliffs."

"There is a large parcel of land there owned by the Cunninghams and several families in my clan call that stretch of Skye home."

"My father's ancestors live there now."

"Then you are indeed kin." He crossed to a tall chest with ornately carved feet, opened the decorative door and lifted the lid of a wooden safe box sitting on the shelf. He slipped her letter inside then returned to his chair. "Zenia tells me the warrior James MacDonald knows all. If you're to live here, then you'll have to cut your ties with him."

"Zenia explained your sister wed the Chief of MacLean and the MacLeans and MacDonalds are at war."

"'Tis a deadly feud that rages between them." He scrubbed a hand over his thick brown beard speckled with gray. "And my sister's enemy is my enemy. I cannae associate with the MacDonalds, no' even one who has aided you."

"I don't wish to cause any problems."

"Good." He nodded. "Then 'tis settled. You are welcome in my home and you will be known as my late cousin's daughter from Skye. That should suffice."

"Will I be able to visit Zenia?"

"As often as you wish." He nodded at Zenia. "I find I am more than intrigued. All will be as you've asked."

"My thanks." Relief poured through her. Arianna would be

well cared for and that was all she could ever ask.

* * * *

Back at her cottage, Zenia and Arianna rejoined James as he paced her front room in a white tunic and tan trews, his daggers sheathed at each wrist and his sword belted at his side. The warrior raised one eyebrow. "What did the earl say, Zenia?"

"He—"

"He said yes." Arianna squealed and jumped into James's arms. The two had formed a close bond over the weeks she'd been confined to her bed. She doubted Arianna would be able to cut all ties with James. 'Twould be an impossibility. "I'm to pack my things and return immediately and I'm allowed to visit Zenia as often as I wish," Arianna told him. "There is only one stipulation I didn't care for."

"And what is that?"

"I'm not allowed to see you. So that means whenever you visit, you'll need to do so in secret."

"Aye, that I can manage." He grinned then slowly frowned. "I came across William again this morn and we fought. I explained to him I gave you my word of protection and that will always stand firm, whether he wishes it or no'." He gestured toward his leather satchel on the tabletop underneath the window. "I bought a gift for you. I wanted you to have it afore I left."

"Is it one of those sugared plums you returned with after your last trip to the village? Those were delicious." She scooped his satchel up and passed it to him.

"Nay, you look inside." He handed the satchel back to her, sat on the wooden bench and patted the space beside him. "Now you'll be out and about, you must take every precaution and this gift will aid you in doing so."

She perched, opened the flap and peered inside. Slowly, reverently, she lifted a tiny wrapped package from within and opened it. She unwrapped the paper and plucked a silver disk free. "Oh, how beautiful. It's a charm."

"Turn it over and read the inscription." James tucked a lock of her blond hair behind her ear.

Arianna did and Zenia leaned forward and smiled as she read the words etched upon it.

Arianna MacLeod Cunningham
DOB: 1569.

"It's perfect and you're so thoughtful." Arianna touched her heart. "I love it." She passed the charm to James. "Can you put it on for me?"

"Of course." He unfastened her necklace, removed the old charm and added the new. "I can look after your old charm if you wish."

"Only if you promise to keep it safe."

"I'll guard it with my life. That I promise you, just as I gave you my word I shall always be here for you." He brought her hands to his lips, kissed her knuckles and stood. "Now, I must be away afore the day is done."

"I hate that you have to leave." She hugged him. "Travel safely and hurry back. I'll be waiting."

"I'll return as often as my duties allow it." He stroked the back of her head and closed his eyes.

The two had formed an unbreakable bond, just as Zenia and Arianna had done. Together, she and James would continue to guard her, their little imp who'd traveled through time.

Chapter 1

Four years later, on the way to Dunvegan Castle, stronghold of clan MacLeod, Isle of Skye, 1590.

Arianna's heartbeat raced as she sat in a birlinn in the dark of night surrounded by the earl, Zenia, and a good twenty of their Cunningham warriors as they sailed along the final seaward stretch toward Dunvegan Castle to join in this year's Highland Games being held on Skye. She longed to experience the week of festivities where the clans gathered and challenged each other, but even more so, to once again be back on land so close to her childhood home.

Overhead, a thick layer of cloud parted and moonlight shimmered through and cast a silvery hue over the forest's treetops edging the coastline. So beautiful. "I've missed this place."

"As have I." Zenia jiggled on the wooden bench seat. "'Tis been twenty-one long years since I was last here. I left no' long after my mother's passing and never returned."

"I'm so glad we've come together." Arianna had begged the earl to allow her to journey here even though his wife was unable to. She'd asked if Zenia could chaperone her and when he'd said yes, she couldn't have been more thrilled. Leaning closer to Zenia, she asked, "Why have you stayed away for so long?"

"I shouldnae have, but I experienced so much loss those last few months I was here. I lived at the castle and my mother was the old chief's healer afore her passing." She lowered her voice further. "Have I ever told you how Cunningham's father, the old earl, came to meet my mother?"

"Only that they met here." Zenia had told her what she'd told no other, the truth of who her father was. Even Cunningham was unaware. All he knew was that Zenia's father had been from his clan.

"The old earl visited his kinsmen here from time to time and when he did he stayed at Dunvegan. 'Twas on one such visit he met my mother and at a time when she was rather young and impressionable."

"That's when they had their affair?"

"Aye, and when it was time for the earl to leave, my mother discovered she was with child and spoke of it to him. She believed herself in love with him, but of course the old earl had no intention of leaving his wife." With a slight tip of her head, she motioned toward the earl as he stood and strode to the center mast and gripped it. "The old earl's son must never know."

"In the future, children are often born out of wedlock and there is no shame."

"Aye, but this isnae the future." With a gentle smile, she snuggled deeper into her red and blue tartan blanket. "Tell me all about Dunvegan Castle as you knew it. I adore hearing you speak of the future."

"I have so many wonderful memories of this place. Dad used to purchase seasonal tickets and brought me here often. I used to listen in on the tours and can likely recite a ton of its history, but there's one secret I must tell you that no one can know."

"What is it?"

"In the mid seventeen-hundreds, the current Chief of MacLeod did something no one ever believed would be possible. He built a landward entrance into Dunvegan."

"Nay." She gasped and sat upright. "But Dunvegan is built on a rock and the loch surrounds most of it. 'Tis inaccessible to reach by land. Surely you jest."

"I promise I'm speaking the truth. There's even a secret tunnel deep underneath the castle that weaves all the way to the land. I haven't been inside it, but it's there and I know it exists."

"A tunnel as well? Oh my." Awe shone in her blue eyes. "What else can you share? What of the MacLeod Fairy Flag? Quite by chance, my mother saw it as a child. Usually 'tis kept well hidden by the chief."

The Fairy Flag was one of their MacLeod clan's most treasured possessions. Decades ago, the fairy princess had fallen in love with the MacLeod chief and begged her father, the fairy king, to allow them to wed. He'd told her she would tire of the human world and wish to return to their people. When she'd declared she wouldn't and once again pleaded, her father instead made her an offer. She could handfast with the MacLeod chief but after a year and a day had passed, she must return to the fairy realm. She and the chief wed and she bore him a son, and when the time came for her to honor her word and return to her people, she asked her handfast husband to promise her that he'd never allow their son to be left alone for if she ever heard him cry, it would tear her heart in two. The chief kept his word and ensured a nursemaid watched over their son at all times, but one day the maid lapsed in her duties and when the princess heard her son's cries, she rushed to him and comforted him then wrapped him in her shawl. When the nursemaid returned, she found the child sleeping peacefully, swathed in a beautiful crimson and yellow patterned cloth. A cloth known from that moment on as the Fairy Flag.

"In the future," Arianna whispered, "the Fairly Flag no

longer remains hidden. It actually sits within a frame in the great hall for all to see, although it's merely a wispy scrap of fabric. Still, I've stood before it and it possesses such an ethereal beauty. Your mother must have been one of the few to have laid eyes on it in this time."

"She was." Zenia breathed deep and sighed as a sad look crossed her face. "I miss her, so much, and Samuel. This return trip to Dunvegan has brought back some poignant memories." Zenia spoke from time to time of Samuel Cunningham, the man she'd been betrothed to. She'd loved him dearly and had never bound herself to another man since. She couldn't, not when Samuel still held her heart.

"Where did your Samuel live?"

"Near the village with his brother until he came of age. Then he moved into the barracks at Dunvegan and trained with my MacLeod kin. Before too long he became one of the old chief's captains. He was a strong and a fierce fighter. 'Twas no' long after we celebrated our betrothal that war broke out on the neighboring Isle of Lewis and Tormod offered our Lewis kin his aid. Both Samuel and my mother sailed to their shores."

"I'm so sorry you lost both of them the way you did. I don't know quite how you dealt with it all."

"Those were some of my darkest days. Tormod told me Mother's death was fast, and Samuel's injury was so severe his breath rattled in and out as he hovered at the edge of death. Tormod did all he could and sent my beloved soaring free, body and soul. The old chief held the same skill as I." She stared out over the blackened waves then wiped a trickling tear from her cheek. "'Twas hard no' having Samuel's body to bury, although Tormod returned with my mother's, her soul at ease."

"Dunvegan lies directly ahead," Cunningham called.

"Oh, we're almost there." Zenia lifted a little to get a better view and Arianna followed suit.

Ahead, Dunvegan rose from the dark like a fortress, its

massive gray towers and fortified walls topped with battlements and guardsmen roaming the ramparts. From the multitude of square windows, candlelight flickered in welcome. Such a glorious sight. "I can't believe I'm about to meet Rory MacLeod. He's known as one of the greatest chiefs of our clan."

"Rory's been to Glencairn over the years, but no' while you've lived there."

"Lower the sail!" Cunningham stood in his great plaid and thick black boots, looking as eager as them all to make landfall. "All to oars."

The warriors plunged their oars into the depths, speeding their birlinn toward the sea-gate. At the edge of the stone landing, two large men waded into the water and as they came abreast of them, each seized a side of the birlinn. Hearty welcomes rang out from the two warriors as they guided the birlinn the last few feet and nestled it next to the stone stairs.

Another warrior walked along the landing toward them, his green eyes glinting with specks of yellow from the flickering torch he held. He offered Arianna his hand. "Watch your step, my lady. The rocks are slippery."

"Thank you." She grasped ahold and he aided her out. Her legs shook from being confined to one position for so long but she stamped her feet and wriggled her toes as they tingled anew.

The earl bounded out onto the landing and eyed the warrior. "We're here at the Chief of MacLeod's invitation. Could you please ensure he's made aware of our—"

"Well, well, if it isnae Cunningham." A towering man descended the stone stairs. Leather trews hugged his thick legs and a buckskin vest molded his broad chest. His dark blond hair, tied back with a strip of leather, gave him a formidable look, as did the battle-axe and sword holstered at his hip. Their Viking heritage couldn't have been more obvious.

"Rory MacLeod." Cunningham stepped up to him. "'Tis good to see you again."

"Welcome to Dunvegan. You and your kin are only the second of the competing clans to arrive. The remainder are due to sail in on the morrow. I've had chambers prepared for you and your kin and pallets laid down in the barracks for your men."

"My thanks." He motioned toward William as he joined them. "William, you've met Rory."

"I have, though 'tis been a while." William adjusted his bow and arrow satchel over one shoulder and shook Rory's hand. At twenty-four, William stood tall, almost eye to eye with Rory.

"Welcome, William. I see my warriors will have some healthy competition during these Games."

"I'm looking forward to the sword challenge in particular."

"Aye, as am I." Rory grinned as Zenia stood and walked to the side of the boat. He offered her a steadying hand as she stepped onto the landing in her blue gown and cloak, her tartan blanket tucked over one arm. "My favorite healer. 'Tis been far too long since you last set foot on Skye, Zenia."

"'Tis wonderful to be home again." Her cheeks flushed a rosy hue. "I hope you'll take care while I'm here no' to climb any trees."

He chuckled. "I shall never live my tree climbing days down with you. How many broken bones of mine did you mend when I was a lad?"

"Far more than I should have, although because of you I did learn how to mend a limb very well."

"That you did."

Cunningham gestured toward Arianna. "Rory, allow me to introduce you to Arianna MacLeod Cunningham. Her late father was a close cousin of mine. Like Zenia, she too has a great love of healing and intends to offer her aid where she can during these Games."

"Another MacLeod. 'Tis good to meet you. Do your kin come from Skye?"

"Yes. I used to live not far from here along the inner channel of the loch toward Dunvegan Village." She dipped her head. "I'm so excited to be here."

"Then come. You must meet my sister, Margaret. She longs for female company. Allow me to lead the way." He strode along the rocky path winding upward, lit by the odd torch staked into the stony ground.

Once they reached the top, they tramped through a darkened passageway and into an inner courtyard. Torches mounted on the stone walls spread their flickering glow while above on the battlements, guardsmen patrolled the ramparts in battle attire and weapons holstered at their sides.

Ahead, the stone entry of the keep beckoned. A boisterous buzz of voices echoed toward her and she took a deep, fortifying breath and entered the great hall. The vaulted room held high wooden beamed rafters, and the plastered walls were covered with beautiful tapestries, of hunting and landscape scenes. Trestle tables were stacked with large platters of cooked meat, roasted vegetables, and bread, while a good hundred warriors in their MacLeod tartan sat on wooden benches enjoying the fine looking fare. Serving maids carried trays holding steaming bowls of stew and bustled about. Never had she seen the castle so alive like this. Hand to her mouth, she turned in a circle, embracing it all. Her father would have loved to have witnessed this. Countless times they'd stood together in this hall then wandered through the public rooms. Her vision blurred and she pushed back threatening tears. Being here again was a dream come true even though it stirred such bittersweet memories.

"I cannae believe we must sit in the same hall as the MacDonalds." William snorted as he gripped his bow.

At the far trestle table, a score of warriors wore the distinctive red, blue and green tartan of the MacDonald clan. She searched amongst the warriors and gasped as one of them rose to his feet. James's great plaid was secured over his chest with a silver pin and belted low at his waist with a leather girdle. His vivid blue gaze, as deep as the ocean, settled on her and her heartbeat fluttered. She hadn't seen him in six agonizing long months, not since his chief had been captured and imprisoned by the king and tossed into Holyrood's tower. He appeared taller, stronger, and his thick biceps bulged as he slid one thumb under his claymore's front belted strap. The hilt of the mighty sword strapped in a baldric across his back gleamed under the candlelit chandelier above.

"Arianna." William's tone was stern as he squeezed her shoulder. "Avert your gaze. Dinnae draw James MacDonald's attention."

"I haven't seen him in so long." Even though she'd tried to meet with James in secret during those times he'd visited, William more often than not learnt of his arrival and the two usually fought. Not once had she been able to stop them.

"He's the enemy and a man you need to steer well clear of." He clenched his teeth.

"He's also one of my guardians whether you wish it or not. Rescuing me from James isn't necessary."

William stroked one finger smoothly down the length of his bow's string line. "Father recently received word from one of my aunt's men that James has not long been at Holyrood House. Apparently he was there to court Rory's cousin, Annie MacLeod. Clearly he seeks an alliance although under the guise of wishing for peace between the clans."

"He intends to wed?" She and James kept nothing from each other. He would have said. "Are you sure?"

"His brother recently spoke vows with another of Rory's close kin. The signs of his clan's intentions are all there." He jerked his head toward the dais where an elegant young lady sat in a corseted cream gown, her pale hair curling in long locks down her back. The fine velvet hugged her trim waist, the gold and red silk ribbons lacing the front an entwining of rich colors.

"That's Rory's sister, Margaret, and now she's eight and ten, I would lay a wager James will be after a contract with her, either by marriage or handfast."

"She's barely of age."

"Women may wed far younger than that. Come." William set a hand at her back and steered her across the room after Rory toward the dais.

The MacLeod chief smiled at his sister. "Margaret, you'll remember the Earl of Glencairn and his son, William."

"I do." Her eyes twinkled as she smiled at them both.

"The earl has also brought his ward, Arianna, and the healer, Zenia MacLeod, as her chaperone. Look after the ladies for me and ensure they know where their chambers are."

"Certainly." Margaret patted the chairs either side of her as Rory offered a seat to Cunningham and William farther along the table. "Come and join me. There are so few women here and I long for female company."

"Thank you." Arianna sat, arranged her sapphire skirts around her and accepted a bowl of stew the serving maid offered her.

Margaret picked up the large pitcher and filled two goblets with warm cider and passed one to her and the other to Zenia. "I've heard so many wonderful tales about you, Zenia, and your late mother. 'Tis intriguing to finally meet you."

"There is little intriguing about me."

"Oh, but I've heard you hold the gifted skill, the same as what my father did." Margaret leaned closer to Zenia as she whispered, "Is that no' the truth?"

"Aye, 'tis the truth. Tormod first taught me all I needed to know about my ability. He was a fine chief and I admired him so." Zenia picked up her spoon and ate a mouthful. "Mmm, this is delicious."

Arianna closed her eyes and breathed in the mouth-watering scent of mutton and vegetables. They'd been traveling for close to a week, eating dried foods and oatcakes. Hot meals had been few and far between and now her belly rumbled. She scooped up the wedge of bread at the side, took a big bite and licked the richly flavored juices as they dribbled from the end. Hearty and delicious.

Margaret selected a morsel of salmon from her trencher and chewed. "I've never traveled as far south as Glencairn. What is the land like there, Arianna?"

"As wild and as beautiful as these isles, although missing the sea since we're some distance inland. It's been an age since I've sailed these waterways."

"Rory has promised to take me to Holyrood House on his next trip this coming spring, although I believe we'll be traveling by road most of the way." She grinned and looked out over the feasting warriors. "It's wonderful to see the clans coming together like this. I so enjoy the Games."

Warriors clanked their tankards together and drank. Food and drink flowed and James nodded at her from his seat next to his men. She smiled and touched her heart. He was so close, yet still so far away, although regardless of William's warning, she would speak to James.

Nothing and no one would stop her.

* * * *

The Cunningham clan had arrived except James had not expected Arianna to be among them. A healthy glow flushed her cheeks and he longed to trace the smattering of sweet freckles across her nose. Six long months had passed since he'd last seen her and he'd never have allowed so much time to pass if it weren't for his clan's feuding with the MacLean of Duart, or his chief's capture by the king's men. He and his brother had fought hard to protect Dunscaith Castle and their lands, but this trip to Dunvegan to participate in the Games had been a necessity, just as his recent trip to Edinburgh to visit his imprisoned chief in the king's tower had been. Donald MacDonald had made his request to him clear. He was to strengthen the ties between the MacDonalds and the MacLeods so the MacLeans would not have such a strong ally against them in this war. If possible, he was to woo Rory's sister, and since it was peace James sought, in many ways he agreed with his chief's plan.

"William Cunningham watches you. So does the earl." Artair, his right hand man, clapped him on the shoulder. "Is there a reason you've already drawn their attention?"

"Possibly." At the dais, Arianna stood, her long golden blond tresses shimmering in the firelight. She eased back into the shadows then disappeared down a darkened hallway. He nodded at Artair and said, "Keep your eye on William and ensure he does no' follow me. I have a wee errand to run."

"Aye, Captain."

He slipped behind a screened doorway and weaved his way around the back passageway toward the hallway Arianna had taken. The gloomy corridor, lit only by the odd candle in an iron wall sconce, remained bare of any other. He slowed near a darkened alcove opposite a half-opened paneled door. This antechamber was one the men used at night when they wished to play a game of cards or converse in private. He'd been in here earlier this eve. With one hand on his sword hilt, he gently, carefully, prodded the door open. It swung wide and Arianna stood in the moonlight beaming through the narrow window. He stepped inside and closed the door. "What are you doing here?" he rasped.

"And hello to you too." Smiling, she set a lit candle in a holder on top of the center table surrounded by six lavishly upholstered chairs.

"There is danger in this meeting."

"There's always danger when you and I meet." She stepped closer and with a soft sigh, pressed her palm against his chest.

Heat radiated from her touch and his fingers twitched with the need to pull her into his arms. He wanted to hold her, as badly as he always did. Instead he shoved his hands behind his back. He was here for peace, which meant forming an alliance with the MacLeods.

Slowly, he stepped back then wandered around the chamber with its bright yellow plastered walls. At the far side, he sat where he could easily watch the door and her.

"Please, I don't like to see you so worried." She crossed to him, her full velvet skirts brushing the polished floorboards. She looked a vision, her gown's square-cut neckline dipping and exposing the swell of her creamy skin. "William told me tonight you might have your sights set on Margaret MacLeod. Is that true?"

"William needs to mind his own business."

"She's only eighteen."

"I'm well aware."

"You intend to offer for her?" She dipped a finger below the embroidered edging of her bodice and freed her silver necklace. She clasped the charm he'd given her firmly in her palm.

"There's a strong possibility, although I've only spoken to her once and that was earlier this eve on my arrival." He eased back in his chair. "My clan's feud with the MacLeans has escalated. My last trip to Edinburgh was to visit my captured chief. I desire peace, Arianna. This war between the clans must come to an end and if an alliance must be made between myself and Margaret, then so be it." He dug into his pocket and gripped her charm, the one he'd promised he'd always keep safe, one he always kept on him.

"I understand your need for peace, but I've missed you."

"As I've missed you." He pressed his elbows to the table. Arianna had made her position clear time and time again. She longed to save her ill father and return to the future, however that could be achieved. There was no place in her life for him. "Does Cunningham still treat you well?"

"Yes. The earl is good to me." She fidgeted with her sapphire gown's long sleeves, tugging the lace hem that draped over her knuckles.

"Then what concerns you? Your agitation is obvious. Speak as you will. You've never held aught back from me afore."

"It's been four years and I'm still here. I'm no closer to returning home than I was at the very beginning."

"Zenia can only call forth her ability if there is a lost soul in need of it."

"I am a lost soul." She swished to his side, hand thumping her chest. "My father is all I have other than you and Zenia, and if you wed another, I'll be forced to let you go too."

"I will always be here for you." Her anguish tore at him and he stood, caught her hand and tugged her closer. Hell, he'd never been able to resist her. "If you've changed your mind and wish to stay in the past, then say the word and I'll pursue you instead." He would, in an instant.

"This isn't my time and it never will be." She leaned her forehead against his chest. "My father needs me."

"I would care for you as none other could."

"I know you would, but I have to halt his death before it happens." She lifted her chin, tears pooling in her eyes. "The disease that takes him can be averted, provided I can get word to him before it does. His life is worth everything to me, and now I'm back on Skye, there must be something more I can do." A lone tear streaked down her cheek and he wiped it away.

"Dinnae cry."

"I feel so torn. I just learnt you're considering another and it hurts."

"We are in a predicament then." He wrapped his arms around her and gently stroked her back. "The feud worsens," he murmured.

"How bad is it?"

"Lachlan MacLean recently attacked my chief's brother and

his clan on the Isle of Islay. He attempted to burn the village of Ardbeg to the ground and when unsuccessful, captured the MacDonald chief's wife and his eldest son. Lachlan MacLean then took to the Rhinns on Islay's western coast and when the MacDonalds of Islay caught up with him, a battle ensued. MacLean was captured and handed over to the king's men, although the MacLeans now seek their revenge against our fellow clansmen. Which means we too must be prepared. Another attack could come at any time."

"I understand your duty is to your clan." She caught his hand, opened his fist and smiled as she gazed at her old charm.

Hell, if he lowered his head, he could claim her lips and the kiss he'd always longed for.

"In the future, one usually marries for love." She traced one finger along his lower lip.

"You must no' touch me so, no' unless you wish for more."

"What I wish for is to have both you and my father, but that will never—" She glanced at the door.

Footsteps echoed down the passageway and swiftly, he tucked Arianna in behind him and clasped his sword. "It appears we're about to have company. Do you wish to take one guess who that might be?"

She sighed. "As much as I adore him, William is like a hound, always scenting his prey. I should leave before he—"

William opened the door and entered, his gaze narrowing on James. "Why am I no' surprised to find you once again meeting in an inappropriate place and time with Arianna?"

"You cannae deny me my duty, and as one of her guardians, I'll meet with her as often as I wish."

"As you always say, and as I always disagree." William bounded forward, sword raised.

* * * *

"No. You two need to stop this." Arianna dived between William and James as they came at each other. Breathing hard, she shoved one hand against each of their chests. "I'm sick of watching you two fight."

"Step aside, Arianna." William's face turned thunderously dark.

"You can't scare me with that look of yours. Honestly, you two are both on the same side when it comes to protecting me. I wish you'd see that."

"You've no need of a MacDonald. His clan are at war with my aunt's MacLean kin. He would gladly take the life of any one of them."

"Only if provoked." James glared at William. "Lower your weapon and I shall do the same. It isnae right to bring Arianna into our disagreement."

William slid his sword away as he eyed her. "I warned you. You're to stay away from him, yet at the first opportunity you defy me."

"You might be at war with James but I'm not, and I have a request to make of him, a very important one which was why I had to see him."

"You can make any request you have need of directly to me."

"Nay, she sought me out, William." James sheathed his blade and crossed his arms. "Speak as you will, Arianna."

"Now I'm back on Skye"—she remained firmly between them—"I'd like to visit my father's home on the land where his ancestors lived, and I'd like you to take me."

"What are your intentions if I allow this?"

"To leave a letter with them, one they can pass along. I've got to do something more to save my father. I fear the reason I'm still here in the past is because none of my letters have yet reached him. Maybe once one does, I'll no longer be a lost soul."

William scoffed. "Father's safe overflows with your letters. One will surely reach him."

James set a hand on her shoulder. "If you wish to deliver

another letter to your father, I'll gladly aid you, but there will be conditions. Although give me some time to consider them all, then we'll speak again."

"Of course. Whatever you ask I'll gladly agree to."

"Good." He strode to the door and glanced over his shoulder at her. "I'll see you on the morrow. Take care this eve."

"I will. Thank you." Excitement bubbled inside her. James never backed down on a promise. She would get her wish, to leave her father another letter. Nothing could have made her happier.

Highlander Heat

Highlander's Castle, Book One
Highlander's Magic, Book Two
Highlander's Charm, Book Three
Highlander's Guardian, Book Four
Highlander's Faerie, Book Five
Highlander's Champion, Book Six

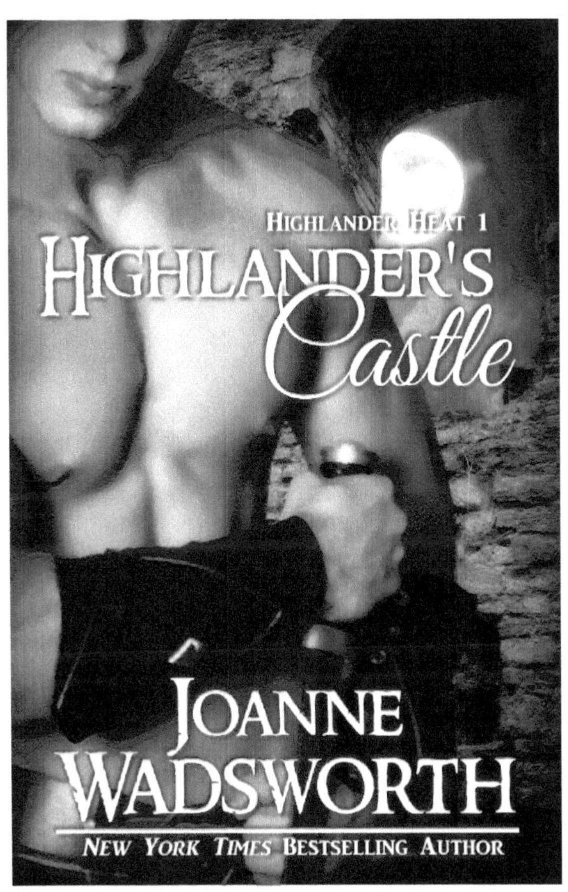

Regency Brides

The Matheson Brothers Continued

Highlander's Kiss, Book Four
Highlander's Heart, Book Five
Highlander's Sword, Book Six

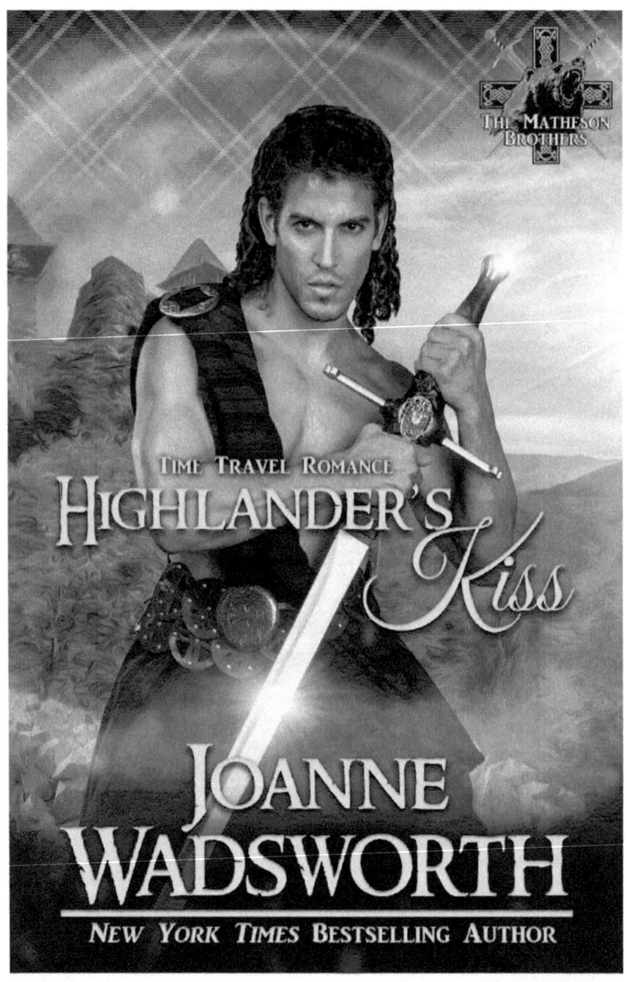

The Matheson Brothers Continued

Highlander's Bride, Book Seven
Highlander's Caress, Book Eight
Highlander's Touch, Book Nine

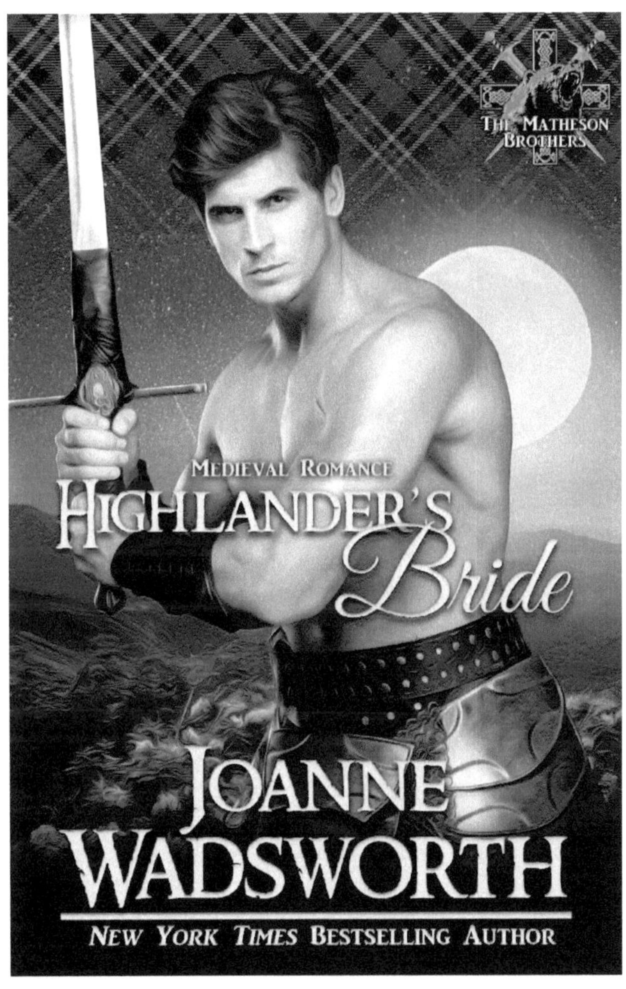

JOANNE WADSWORTH

The Matheson Brothers Continued

Highlander's Shifter, Book Ten
Highlander's Claim, Book Eleven
Highlander's Courage, Book Twelve
Highlander's Mermaid, Book Thirteen

Princesses of Myth

Protector, Book One
Warrior, Book Two
Hunter (Short Story - Included in Warrior, Book Two)
Enchanter, Book Three
Healer, Book Four
Chaser, Book Five

BILLIONAIRE BODYGUARD
Attraction
BILLIONAIRE BODYGUARDS BOOK ONE
JOANNE
WADSWORTH
NEW YORK TIMES BESTSELLING AUTHOR

JOANNE WADSWORTH

Joanne Wadsworth is a *New York Times* and *USA Today* Bestselling Author who adores getting lost in the world of romance, no matter what era in time that might be. Hot alpha Highlanders hound her, demanding their stories are told and she's devoted to ensuring they meet their match, whether that be with a feisty lass from the present or far in the past.

Living on a tiny island at the bottom of the world, she calls New Zealand home. Big-dreamer, hoarder of chocolate, and addicted to juicy watermelons since the age of five, she chases after her four energetic children and has her own hunky hubby on the side.

So come and join in all the fun, because this kiwi girl promises to give you her "Hot-Highlander" oath, to bring you a heart-pounding, sexy adventure from the moment you turn the first page. This is where romance meets fantasy and adventure…

To learn more about Joanne and her works, visit
http://www.joannewadsworth.com